D1442792

— Looking for —
Jamie Bridger

~ Looking for ~
Jamie Bridger

Nancy Springer

Dial Books for Young Readers
New York

Published by Dial Books for Young Readers
A Division of Penguin Books USA Inc.
375 Hudson Street
New York, New York 10014

Designed by Julie Rauer
Printed in the U.S.A.
First Edition
1 3 5 7 9 10 8 6 4 2

Library of Congress Cataloging in Publication Data
Springer, Nancy.
Looking for Jamie Bridger / Nancy Springer.
p. cm.
Summary: Fourteen-year-old Jamie Bridger
is determined to find out who her real parents were in
spite of opposition from the grandparents who raised her,
but her search ends in a bittersweet discovery.
ISBN 0-8037-1773-3
[1. Parents—Fiction. 2. Grandparents—Fiction.
3. Mental illness—Fiction. 4. Homosexuality—Fiction.] I. Title.
PZ7.S76846Lo 1995 [Fic]—dc20 94-25484 CIP AC

— Looking for —
Jamie Bridger

Chapter

1

"I just want to know, that's all," Jamie said, careful not to raise her voice. Grandma was like a big timid flower, filling the house with the good smells of her cleaning and cooking, seldom going out. Her petals were frail. When voices rose, Lily Bridger tended to droop, and curl at the edges, and fall to pieces. Therefore, though it was hard for a kid who had been known to yell from the art room clear down to the girl's gym in school, Jamie kept her voice down. She spoke softly and tried to reason with Grandma.

"It's pretty basic, knowing who your own parents are," she said. "Even adopted kids know who their parents are."

"You're not adopted!" Grandma's mouth quivered and her hands fumbled with the early strawberries she was slicing. It must have been the wrong thing to say. Damn, double damn. Now Grandma was upset.

Jamie felt her head start to pound with frustration but

managed to keep her voice gentle. "Of course I'm not adopted. Good grief, I look just like you." Jamie had a wide freckled face like her grandmother's, a cleft chin like Grandpa's, blue eyes like both of them. Anybody could tell they were related. "I never said I was adopted." Jamie pushed her school books to one side, because the dowdy old kitchen was small, like the dowdy old rented house, and Grandma needed table space for dinner preparations. "Do you want me to get a pie crust ready?"

"No. Not if you are going to say such awful things." Grandma snatched a posy-print towel and wiped her hands on it, sniffling, working herself up to a crying fit.

"It's not awful, Grandma! It's natural. I just want—" Now Jamie heard her own voice start to shake with wanting; she was getting emotional the way Grandma did, and she hated that. She forced herself to say steadily, "I just want to know who my parents are."

"I raised you, isn't that good enough?" Grandma cried. Chin jerking, she marched to the old gas stove and started slamming pots around without accomplishing anything. "I fed you, I made smocked dresses for you, I—"

Just this once, Jamie promised herself, *I am not going to back down.* No matter how much Grandma cried, no matter how mad Grandpa got when he came home and found Grandma in a snit fit.

"—taught you how to tie your shoes, I—"

I have to find out. I can't go on not knowing who I am. Jamie was fourteen, closer to fifteen, already a freshman in high school. In a few years she would be able to drive a car, vote—she would be an adult. She had to get a handle on this parent thing.

8

"—made you real chicken soup when you were sick, bought you peppermints—"

Grandma wore her hair in braids pinned tight to her head. When she was little, Jamie had loved to watch Grandma brush her hair and do her braids. Grandma's long hair had never been cut, not once in her whole life, and now it was like a history of Grandma, mouse brown at the tips, pure white at the roots. Braided and piled on her head, it made Grandma look both old-fashioned and girlishly young, with the brown hiding the white. But right now the white was showing. As always when Grandma fell apart, her braids were coming loose, coiling away from her head.

"—and ice cream and coloring books—"

"I know," Jamie said. "I love you." This was true.

Her grandmother wheeled around to face her, braids swinging, rose-print skirt swinging from her wide hips, tears running down her wide, plain face. She wailed, "So what do you need a mother for?"

Jamie looked straight back, assessing her own commitment to what she wanted—no, what she needed. Yes, she really was determined enough to keep pushing. This time she was not going to give in, and knowing it made her very calm, almost cold. "Is that what I'm likely to find? A mother?" she demanded. "A daughter of yours, I mean, who had me?"

Lily stared back at her without moving even to sob.

"Just tell me that much," Jamie urged. "Please." She had never gotten even this far before. "You had a daughter? A son?" Much later, looking back, she knew she should have asked other questions: You had a child you

9

have not seen in fourteen years? You had a child whose pictures are not in the photo album? You had a child you never talk about? But she did not ask those questions. She barely dared to think them, because then she had to think . . . no. It was just not possible. Grandma had a child she had . . . disowned? But Grandma would never do that. If Grandma could do that to anyone, then she could do it to . . .

No. That's stupid. She loves me.

But Jamie felt a catlike, secret fear. She needed to know who her parents were. She needed parents.

Just in case . . . something happened.

Jamie insisted, "You had a daughter who got in trouble? Or was it a son? Did you have a son who got a girl—"

She stopped because of the look on her grandmother's face, which frightened her. But why? Lily did not seem the least bit angry, or even weepy anymore. Instead, she had suddenly become totally serene.

"I don't remember," Lily said.

"Grandma, *please.*"

"I'm sorry, honey, I just don't remember." Grandma came back to the table, reached for the flour canister and started to measure and sift for pie crust, her movements smooth and deft, as if not a thing were wrong. "That was a long time ago," she added.

Jamie stumbled to her feet, tried to speak calmly yet found herself shouting. "You have to remember!" How could anyone not remember her own child?

But Grandmother—was this Grandma, Lily who so easily wilted? Unperturbed by Jamie's shouting, she gave her a sweet, rueful smile. "I am so forgetful these days," she said.

"My parents," Jamie whispered. "I need to know who my parents were."

Grandma stood there briskly mixing dough, shaking her head at herself, looking puzzled and cheerful. "Maybe the angels brought you," she said. "You were such a beautiful baby. And now you're a beautiful, beautiful girl."

Jamie knew Grandma meant this, but it was not true, and no help. She wanted to cry. She wanted to stamp her feet and scream. She stood there.

Grandma said softly, "I remember thinking how beautiful you were, dressing you to bring you home. You were like peaches and cream. I wished I had a pink bunting for you, but all I had was blue."

The remembering look on Grandma's face was as if a door had opened, just for a flash. Jamie cried, "Home from where?"

But she had spoken too loudly. Her grandmother went blank and blinked at her. "Why, I don't know, honey child. I don't remember. That was fourteen years ago."

The dowdy house was one of many, ranked in rows along narrow streets, standing tall and narrow like an old horse's brown teeth. Originally built by a coal company, these houses were never meant to be pretty, and they were not. Dexter, Pennsylvania, was not a pretty town. Therefore it did not look at other towns too much. Far from anywhere, shut off by mountains, Dexter ignored a lot that had changed outside. Jamie was not the only high-school girl in Dexter who was not allowed to date or wear bicycling

11

tights or get her ears pierced or use makeup or stay out after dark. Dexter had a tradition of hiding its daughters. The houses were built so that the daughter in the back upstairs bedroom had to walk through her parents' room to get out. Jamie's grandpa's rules did not make her so very different.

But she felt different, because she liked to read, and she loved to draw, and she had no parents, only dreams. And memories so vague, they might as well have been dreams—hazy memories of a house very different than any house in Dexter. A house with a bay window, lots of windows, a house filled with light, with a half-moon glass over the front door and a porch thickly edged with fancy railings, fringed like a cowboy's white shirt. Once in Jamie's very early life, evidently, there had been a place that was not Dexter, and she dreamed of going there. It was quite possibly the place where her parents were.

"I could scream," Jamie complained to her friend Kate.

"Chill out, Jame. Your grandma is sweet." Standing behind Jamie, Kate was trying to do something with Jamie's hair. Not that it would help, but being fussed over felt good. One of these times Jamie and Kate were going to give each other canned-frosting-and-shaving-cream facials, and it would not be the craziest thing they had ever done together. Having a best friend who lived right next door was the best part of Jamie's life. When she was at Kate's house, Jamie felt real, as if she could be herself, when at home she felt—what? Was that silent, patient Jamie less real? Would the real Jamie Bridger please stand up?

No, forget standing up. She sagged down in Kate's bedroom chair and relaxed.

"How old was I when we moved here, about four?" she asked with her eyes closed.

"Five. Same as me." They had started kindergarten together. "You getting forgetful in your old age?" Kate teased.

"Not really. I knew I was four or five. So it's been, like, ten years?"

"Like, yeah. You getting nostalgic too?"

The teasing was gentle. Kate's hands were gentle on her head. Jamie smiled but said, "I keep asking my grandmother where we lived before. Can you believe she doesn't remember?"

Holding Jamie's hair straight up in the air with one hand, Kate came around to the front of the chair and studied Jamie. Kate changed future careers about once a month, and this month she was going to be a hair designer, so she was practicing analyzing the shapes of faces. She said, "I think it would look cool if you got it cut real short and wore it kind of wild on top."

"Give me a break." Jamie felt sure no hairstyle could make her look attractive, ever. Pretty girls had oval faces like Kate's, not square ones. "Does it make sense to you that Grandma wouldn't even remember the name of the town where we lived when I was little? She ought to remember the name of the town where she lived before she moved here!"

"Yes," Kate admitted, letting go of Jamie's hair, which fell straight down around her ears. If something was wrong with Grandma Bridger, it was a problem for Kate too, because Kate had no grandparents of her own; Lily was Kate's "Mamaw." Therefore, Kate started paying attention and sat on the edge of her bed to face Jamie. "Mamaw ought to remember that. Is she getting, you know, too old?"

"Senile? I don't think so. It's not like she's changed." Grandma had always been the same person, the one who bloomed in the kitchen, shriveled outside the house.

"Is she just saying she doesn't remember? Because she doesn't want to tell you things?"

"That's what I used to think. But today—" Jamie sat up, feeling herself go tense and quivery just thinking back to the conversation in the kitchen. "Today all of a sudden I felt like, it's for real, she honest to God does not remember, you know? She doesn't remember—anything." Jamie hunched her shoulders and shivered. "She forgets who her own kid was who had me."

Kate looked as shocked as Jamie felt. "What?!"

"I mean it. I asked her if it was a son or a daughter, and she said she can't remember. And she meant it. I mean, I just know she meant it. She really has forgotten."

"Whoa." Kate's eyes had gone huge. "That's spooky."

"It's crazy, is what it is! She scares me."

"Aw, c'mon. You can't be scared of your grandma."

"I was for a minute. All of a sudden I realized I was standing there talking to a crazy person."

"Maybe not really. People that age, a lot of them are funny." Kate looked off to one side the way she always did when she was thinking hard, and Jamie watched her. It did not bother Jamie that Kate was beautiful, with large dark eyes and almost a fashion-model face and spectacular

14

hair, long and thick and pure black, swinging to her waist. If somebody had to be gorgeous, Jamie was glad it was Kate. She was going to do a portrait of Kate someday, when she got better at drawing humans. Right now, she was only good at drawing wild animals, deer and foxes and raccoons and such.

"First of all, your grandma is nice," Kate said slowly. "Maybe too nice. She spends her whole life doing things for other people, you know what I mean?"

Jamie nodded. She sometimes wished her grandma would get a life, like Kate's mother, who was Faye Garibay, County Commissioner. But on the other hand, she knew Kate sometimes wished her mother would bake strawberry pie.

"Second of all, she probably has some weird ideas, you know? Like, my grandmother would be about the same age if she was alive, and there were things she never told my mom. Dumb things, like Aunt Millie dyed her hair."

"So my grandmother is hiding something," Jamie grumbled. "So what else is new?"

"Well, it was a big deal back then if somebody had a baby when they weren't supposed to! Maybe your grandma is more ashamed than you can imagine."

This made some sense. Having a baby involved sex, and Grandma and Grandpa seemed scared to death of sex. Actually, they were scared of lots of things, like sunbathing, canasta, and popular music, all of which were supposed to shortcut a person straight to hell. But sex was worst of all. Grandpa used to be a kind of tent-revival preacher, and whatever Grandpa thought, Grandma thought the same, so between the two of them they never

15

even said the word "sex." Whenever Jamie had sex education in school, she had to look up all the words. She knew better than to ask at home. Once, hearing Grandpa refer to a boy walking past the house as a "pervert" and a "Godless homosexual," she had asked what he meant, and ended up grounded for a week. To Grandma and Grandpa, anything having to do with sex was unspeakably bad.

But no, it did not entirely make sense. Jamie said, "She still ought to be able to remember. I can't imagine being so ashamed that you actually can't remember."

"Oh, boogers, I don't know." Kate got up and started to comb Jamie's hair again. Her hands made hard, jerky movements at first, but then they relaxed and played lightly around Jamie's head. "You've got a nice, symmetrical head and face," she said to Jamie after a while.

"What's that mean? Both my eyes aren't on the same side of my big fat nose?"

Kate, who hardly ever got angry, slammed down the comb. "Jamie Lee, you make me so mad, you have such a rotten negative attitude about yourself! Who says there is only one way to be pretty?"

Jamie's mouth jolted open.

"If you would smile once in a while!" Kate fumed. "You have the greatest smile."

When she managed to get her mouth under control Jamie said, "Don't mind me. I'm just bummed about stuff."

Kate knew what that meant: Jamie was on a wanting-parents jag again. "You remind me of a dog chasing cars," Kate grumbled. "What's it going to do if it catches one?

It's dumb. It's kind of like me wishing I had grandparents. What are you going to do with parents if you find them?"

"I—I don't know. Write letters. Be a pen pal. Swap pictures, send Christmas cards, I don't know!" Jamie felt herself clouding up to cry, but so what. She could cry in front of Kate if she had to. "It's not what Grandma thinks, it's not that I want a mother so much." Jamie had been mothered pretty well. Also, she had doubts about her mother: *She had to know I was born. Why did she give me away? Didn't she want me?* But there was a chance her father had not known about her, and might have wanted her very much if he did. "Mostly I think I want a father."

"Oh." Kate's voice gentled, and she came around and sat on the bed again. "I get it."

"Yeah." Jamie's grandfather was not exactly Mr. Teddy-Bear Hugs.

"You have in mind a young, cute father, or what?"

In her daydreams Jamie did. In her daydreams her father was wonderful in every way, and he came to Dexter in a white Ferrari to take her away. But she did not feel like admitting any of this. "I don't care as long as he likes me." Grandpa had always let her know that being a girl was a mistake.

"Don't count on anything."

"I'm not."

"Well, look." Kate turned helpful. "How much your grandmother really forgets is kind of beside the point, which is, she's not going to tell you anything."

Time to face it. "Yeah."

"So how else can you find out? Can you send for your birth certificate or something?"

"How?"

"I dunno."

"Would they even give it to me? I'm a kid."

"I dunno. You could try."

"I could hire a private detective too, if I had a few thousand dollars."

Kate heard the sarcasm in Jamie's voice and sighed. "Don't be that way."

Jamie said nothing, because she knew what she actually had to do, and she was not looking forward to it. Eating raw liver would have been an attractive alternative.

Kate knew too. "You thinking of asking your grandfather?"

"Yeah," Jamie said.

Chapter

2

"I've never really gotten over it." On a footbridge in Central Park the man looked down into gray water as he spoke. He had a square face, a cleft chin, freckles, warm blue eyes, wide shoulders, a wide, sweet smile—he was handsome in his own way. "Here I am, thirty-one, almost thirty-two, and I still hurt when I think about it."

"We all get that way sometimes," his friend said. The two of them stood on the arch of the bridge, leaning over the railing, watching the ripples.

"They locked me out," the square-faced man said. "Dad took me by the arms and flung me out the door. It was January, for God's sake—Mom wanted to give me a coat but Dad wouldn't let her. He told her to put it away, and she did. He told her to close the door and lock it, and she did. I damn near froze."

"What did you do?"

"Stole a piece of rug out of the back of somebody's van and wrapped it around me and spent the night in a toolshed trying not to cry." The man shivered and shook his head, thinking about it. "I was sixteen years old."

"Did you go back and try—"

"Yes, the next morning, and they wouldn't let me in! I tried for days. Stayed with this friend and that friend, tried phoning—they hung up on me. Tried writing a letter, pounding on the door, sitting on the front steps, nothing worked. Mom looked out the window at me once, but that was all. They never spoke to me again."

His friend gave him a startled look. "Still?"

"Still. I couldn't keep sitting on their porch—"

"Well, no."

"—I just couldn't take it anymore. So I found a burger-flipping job and a place to stay, and then I had a chance to move to the city, and if I wanted any kind of decent job I had to finish school—anyhow, it was a few years before I felt able to go back there, and when I did, they were gone."

"Gone?"

"Gone. Moved away. No forwarding address."

"Bridger, there's ways to—"

"I tried, man! I talked with all the neighbors, all my friends, half the people in that town. Nobody knew where they went. They didn't leave any messages with anyone. I hired a missing-persons guy, and he couldn't find them either, and the reason why, he said, was because they didn't want to be found. They cut themselves off." He ducked his head, and his voice went ragged. "They locked me out for good."

"That's rough." The friend spoke softly, his eyes worried. "Most of us, if we fight with our families, things change in time. We grow up, they get older, they accept, we get back together."

"Yeah. I know."

"I can't believe—I can't believe they won't come around eventually. Have you left word with friends? So if your parents come looking they can find you?"

Bridger shook his head. "It's no use."

"You ought to, man. So you'll know you've done everything you can. Do you keep in touch with your high school?"

"I didn't even graduate!"

"You're still a member of the class. You should get in touch with the reunion committee. You'd be surprised how going home, even to a high-school reunion, can help you feel better."

Bridger pushed himself away from the bridge railing and looked up, at the trees, at the skyscrapers towering beyond them. He squared his shoulders and looked thoughtfully at his companion. "It's not like I go around feeling rotten all the time," he said. "I've got a life."

"But?"

"But . . . I wonder about Mom sometimes, how she is. Back then I was mad, I felt like she should have stood up for me—but now I can see, she was a victim, you know? It was like he had her brainwashed. She always did whatever he told her. Always."

"Nice guy," the friend said.

"Actually, in a weird way he was nice to her, most of the time. He was kind to her. Like she was a child."

"As long as she did exactly what he told her."

"Yes."

21

"And if she didn't?"

"As far as I know she's never dared to find out."
Bridger sighed and turned to walk back to the streets of
the city. "She's probably still with him, she's probably still
jumping when he calls. I disobeyed, and she saw what
happened to me."

Jamie waited until Saturday, when Grandpa would be a
little more approachable than he was on weekday eve-
nings. As Grandma put it, he "worked too hard" at the
artificial-tooth factory where he was a plastics specialist.

Jamie waited until after Grandpa had taken Grandma
grocery shopping. (Grandma did not drive.) She waited
until after he had taken down the heavy, old-fashioned
wooden storm windows and put screens in—by himself,
not allowing Jamie or Grandma to help, because it was
not women's work. Grandpa had quite definite ideas of
what men were supposed to accomplish and what women
were supposed to do. You would never see him in the
kitchen except to eat. That was fine with Jamie most days,
because she could go to the kitchen to stay away from
him—it worked almost as well as taking one of her long
walks in the woods. This day, though, she stayed around
the house, and waited, and watched her grandfather from
the kitchen door.

She waited until he had taken off his work boots and
was sitting on the porch while Grandma fixed dinner—
stewed chicken with gravy, his favorite. She waited until
she was afraid she would chicken out if she waited any
longer.

Grandpa was an egg-shaped person, but not soft.

Hard-boiled. His skin stretched almost hairless over the hardness of his head. He seldom said much. Jamie could not remember that he had ever hugged her or kissed her.

She had thought about this interview, and had settled on an approach. "Grandpa," she said, sitting on a porch chair next to him, "I need your help with something." She had asked him for help with a science project once, and he had been pleased to offer suggestions.

This time, though, he gave her a flat stare, like a dead fish, and she knew he saw through her. Damn, he was smart, about plastics and lots of other things. He would have been an executive at the tooth plant except nobody liked him.

"You had better go set the table for your grandmother," he said, not unkindly. Warning her gently: Be a good girl, back off. Usually Jamie would have heeded the warning. But she had promised herself that this time she was not going to back off.

"Grandpa," she said, "it's about my parents."

He sat up straight on his metal porch chair. *"Go,"* he warned, sternly this time. "Do what I told you."

"Grandpa, please. I—"

"No!" He roared the word, and his entire hairless head flushed strawberry red. "You will not—"

"I need to know—"

Grandpa lurched up. "You *shall* be silent! You *shall* not speak of parents!" He shouted so loud, the words stretched out of shape, were hard to understand. Neighbors working in their yards turned around to see what was happening. Grandma came scuttling out of the kitchen and hurried toward Jamie, her face white as flour. Jamie knew why. She felt frightened pale herself by her grandfather's rage. She had never seen him so enraged. The force of his shouting stunned her. She could not move or speak.

"You *shall* not think of those Godless fornicators!" He was roaring. "You *shall* not harbor those thoughts. You have nothing to do with the—the slut and the goat who begot you. They were evil people, *evil*, I tell you. Your parents were sensual, evil, lewd—" Grandpa had to stop shouting and pant for breath. His chest wheezed and the whites of his eyes showed. Sweat broke out on his reddened forehead.

"Cletus!" Grandma pushed Jamie aside and laid shaky hands on his forearm. "Come inside, dear, you're upset. Jamie didn't mean to upset you. She doesn't understand, she didn't know. You won't ever mention such people to your grandfather again, will you, sweetie?" The look Grandma gave her was a panicky appeal. "Open the door for your grandpa. There. Come in and sit down, Cletus, dinner's almost ready. Jamie, set the table, please."

She did so, quickly, aware that her grandmother was rescuing her. Lily rattled pots frantically at the stove, getting dinner into serving dishes at top speed. Grandpa sat in his place at the head of the table and panted, still trying to catch his breath. Careful not to look at him, Jamie felt the words he had shouted crawling up her spine. Evil? Her mother, her father, evil? It was a double-edged knife of a word, cutting at Grandpa as much as anyone. But still, what if her father was not the prince-on-a-white-horse person she wanted to find? What if he was a macho jerk, the kind to get a woman pregnant and walk away? Or what if her mother was a, well, a slut?

Maybe her grandparents were stonewalling her for a good reason. The way Grandma seemed so frightened, Grandpa so enraged—maybe there was something awful waiting out there. Maybe she had better just give up this idea of finding her parents.

"There," Grandma sang, scooting a dish of cranberry relish to the table. "We're all ready."

"I want applesauce," Grandpa said.

"Yes, Daddy." Grandma often called him Daddy, and she was not joking when she said it. She whisked to the refrigerator, spooned him a side dish of applesauce, sprinkled cinnamon on top, and set it at his place.

"Do we have pickles?"

"Yes, Daddy." Grandma fetched a jar of sweet gherkins from the cupboard and set it on the table. Grandpa scowled.

"Put them in a dish, for heaven's sake."

Grandma spooned pickles into a pressed-glass serving dish and set it next to the applesauce.

"I want garlic pickles next time we go to the store."

Grandma wrote the requisition on her grocery list, then stood awaiting further orders.

"Sit down, Lil, before everything gets cold."

"Yes, Daddy." Grandma sat. Jamie had already taken her place. Her grandfather did not look at her as he folded his big-knuckled hands, inclined his bald head, and recited a monotone blessing.

Listening with downturned eyes, Jamie felt only impatience. Kate's family held hands around the supper table when they prayed, and when Jamie was there she held hands with them, and felt as if a blessing were really hap-

25

pening. But coming from Grandpa, the prayer was only words to her.

When he had said grace, Grandpa proceeded to build himself his stewed chicken supper. Jamie sat and frankly stared. She had watched him do this hundreds of times and still could not quite believe it. First he put down a waffle, not a frozen waffle from the grocery store but a thick, fresh homemade waffle as big as his plate. He buttered it—Grandpa required real butter; no margarine was allowed. Then he mounded hot mashed potatoes on top of the waffle. He made a crater in the potato mound and put a chunk of butter there. Then he piled a mess of Grandma's hot homemade egg noodles on top of the potatoes. He buttered them. Then he spooned stuffing on top of that. Finally, he poured about a pound of stewed chicken in gravy all over everything. Luckily, the old-fashioned dinner plates were wide and deep enough to hold all this.

Rapidly and methodically, working his way around the plate in wedge-shaped sections, Grandpa ate. Grandma took a little chicken and some noodles. Jamie had never felt less like eating, but knew better than to say so. She put chicken gravy on a little stuffing, and made herself swallow some of it.

No one said anything, but then, no one ever did say much at dinner. Grandpa was serious about his dinner. Maybe tonight he was angry, ignoring her. Jamie could not tell for sure, but she did not desperately care. She had given up caring much about her grandpa or whether he liked her. It was other thoughts that sat like a brick in her stomach and kept her from eating.

Where are my parents? Jamie was thinking. *Forget the daydream crap—they probably both know about me. Why hasn't either of them ever come to see me? What kind of people are they?*

"Get me something to drink," Grandpa told Grandma.

She got up, poured him a glass of ice water from the refrigerator bottle, brought it to him, and sat down again.

"You're a good girl, Lil." Mellowed now by stewed chicken and gravy, Grandpa smiled at her and patted her hand.

"Thank you, Daddy." She smiled back at him. "Rhubarb pie for dessert."

"Not right now." He had eaten everything on his plate and looked uncomfortable. Well, no wonder.

Effortlessly Grandma switched from being his adoring little girl to being his doting mother. "Then you just go sit in your chair, Cletus."

He waddled to the recliner in the living room, lay back with a groan, and closed his eyes. Soon he would be snoring.

In the kitchen Jamie helped Grandma clear away the dinner things, then started washing the dishes. There were a lot of them, especially pots, what with cooking waffles, and potatoes, and noodles, and chicken, and gravy. What a dumb meal. What a typical Bridger meal. What a weird meal. Jamie had gone numb inside, and everything seemed to be boringly normal, yet at the same time very strange.

"Well, gee, Grandma," Jamie said, trying to joke, "if I can't have parents, can I at least have a puppy?"

Wiping the stove, Grandma gave her a startled glance.

"Or a pony?"

"Jamie, you know the lease says no pets." If Grandma had a sense of humor, Jamie had never been able to locate it.

"A hamster? They wouldn't notice a hamster."

"Jamie, please." Grandma turned toward her and lowered her voice to a desperate whisper. "You mustn't say things that might annoy your grandfather. You simply must not. Promise me."

Jamie felt a sudden urgent need to get out of there. "May I go see Katie? Take her some pie?" Jamie doubted that any of the Garibays actually liked rhubarb pie, but it was an excuse to get out. Out of the Bridger house, where Jamie always felt somehow fake.

A fake what? If she wasn't herself, who was she? Life was weird.

"Promise me," Grandma insisted.

"Grandma, I can't promise never in my life to annoy Grandpa!"

"But you have to!" Grandma's lower lip was trembling. "You don't understand what might happen."

Bone-tired, Jamie did not want to know what that meant. "Don't cry," she complained, and as if offering a different toy to a child, she tried distracting Grandma. "It's time for the news."

"Oh, dear. Go wake your grandfather." Grandpa hated to miss the news.

Jamie dried her hands and walked into the living room. She heard the tall old floor clock ticking. The room was oddly quiet, and in a moment she understood why. There Grandpa lay on his recliner with his mouth sagging open, a string of drool at one corner, but for a change he was not snoring.

"Grandpa." Jamie gently touched his elbow. "Grandpa." She joggled his arm a little.

Then she let go and backed up, staring. He had not moved.

He absolutely had not moved.

He absolutely was not moving. He was not breathing.

It was the idea and the suddenness of the thing that made her scream, not any sense of loss. It was the shock of finding death in the living room while the waffle iron was still soaking in the kitchen sink. It was the plastic feel of her grandfather's arm when she had touched him. "Ma!" Jamie screamed as if she were about two years old—and when had she ever called Grandma just Ma? *"Grandma!"*

Her grandmother came running in and looked. Grandpa's color was strange, gray, and he lay so still he seemed to suck all the life out of the room, turning it gray along with him. "Cletus," Grandma said. "Daddy. Oh, no. No!" She fell to the floor, lily white.

Jamie had to step over her fainting grandmother to get to the phone. It was up to her to dial 911. It was up to her to coax Grandma back to consciousness. It was up to her to let in the police and medics when they came. It was up to her to hold Grandma while Grandma cried. She did those things because there was no one else to do them.

There was no one now to take care of this frail old Lily flower but Jamie.

Chapter

3

"I never knew having a dead person was such a hassle," Jamie whispered to Kate the next day while Grandma was upstairs resting. "It's a mess."

"You mean, like, choosing a coffin and all that?"

"I mean, the whole stupid thing! How are we supposed to pay for a funeral? Everything was in his name. We can't get money out of the bank because it's all in Grandpa's name, savings, checking account, everything. We can't even use my savings account—it has his name on it. We can't get a loan, because Grandma doesn't know how much she has coming to her. She doesn't know what Grandpa said in his will. She doesn't even know where it is. And she doesn't have any money of her own. None."

Kate listened with her mouth open. "You mean, like, not even spending money? In her purse?"

"No! She never carried money. He took care of that. All we have is what was in his wallet when he died."

"Let me guess," Kate said. "Fifty dollars and some odd cents."

"Close enough." Jamie's voice rose. "Why did he have to go and put everything in his name?"

"Your grandpa was kind of a control freak."

"Nooooo. He was only the most retentive person I ever met." No wonder he died of heart failure. *He died happy,* Jamie thought sourly. *In complete control of his dinner and my life.*

Kate asked, "So what are you going to do until it gets straightened out? You got, like, a rich uncle or anything?"

"I don't have *any* uncles. That's another thing." Jamie shook her head, wishing it would all just go away, the strangers with their papers and their questions, her grandmother's pain. "I never knew we were so, uh, different. Like, most people have relatives?"

"Well, yeah," Kate drawled.

"Well, we don't. No aunts, no uncles, no cousins, no in-laws, no anybodies. Nobody to notify. Nobody to come to the funeral."

No pastor. No church. None of the churches in Dexter were strict enough to suit Grandpa—or that was his excuse. Really, Jamie figured, he wasn't the kind to sit and listen to somebody else preach and tell him what to do. He needed to have his own religion, under his own control.

So what did he have now? Nothing. People were being nice, but nobody really cared that he was gone.

"I'll be there," Kate said, "to keep you company." She peered at Jamie. "You want me to stay with you tonight? You look a little tired."

"Could you?" Jamie had not thought she needed to cry, but suddenly she was teary-eyed. "Thanks," she managed to say. "I didn't sleep at all last night."

"You sleep tonight and I'll help Mamaw if she needs anything. You been eating?"

"Oh, yeah." The kitchen was full of tempting food brought by neighbors and people who had worked with Mr. Bridger. The refrigerator shelves were stacked with casseroles. Cakes and fancy breads sat on the table and countertops. Kate had just added the Garibay contribution, a Virginia spiral-cut ham with honey-mustard glaze. Jamie pulled off a morsel and tasted it—yum, delicious. "I'm eating okay. I'm not really that upset. Well, maybe I am, a little." Jamie rolled her eyes at her own mixed feelings about her grandfather.

Bless Kate—she understood immediately and smiled to let Jamie know it was all right. "He was kind of a bumhead," she said.

"He was a *total* bumhead. I am so mad at him." He had withheld from her all the things she needed to know, and now he was dead, and he would lie smirking in his coffin with all her secrets inside him.

Yet Jamie felt guilty, as if she had killed him. If she hadn't made him yell and strain his heart, might he still be alive?

"It was his own stupid fault if he never went to a doctor," Kate said, reading Jamie's thought again.

"I feel bad because I didn't always—you know. I didn't like him much."

"Oh, well, who could? Never mind. Have a ham sandwich before somebody needs you for something."

Jamie had seen her friend eyeing the meat hungrily. "You have something. Good grief, look at all this food. Help me out."

"Well . . . only if you have some too."

They both piled ham and Swiss cheese on somebody's home-baked marble bread, then munched silently. They were slicing into pineapple upside-down cake when there was a slow old sound in the next room and Grandma shuffled in.

"Mamaw." Kate got up and hugged her. Grandma hugged back a little, but mostly just leaned against Kate and rested her head on Kate's shoulder.

"Katie," she murmured. "Sweetie. Don't ever get old and married and stupid."

Jamie saw Kate's eyes widen. Kate did not know what to say. "Have some cake, Grandma?" Jamie offered, though she knew it was no use.

"No, thank you, honey. I can't—"

For about the dozenth time that day, the phone rang. Jamie answered it and sighed when she learned it was not something she could handle.

"Grandma, can you talk to this lady? She needs some information for the obituary."

"Oh, dear." Her slippers dragging on the linoleum, Grandma went to the phone.

Sitting at the table with Kate, Jamie heard only the Bridger end of the conversation. "Yes . . . yes, he died at home. Six P.M. He was sixty-four; he would have retired next year . . . pardon?" Grandma was faltering her way through this, but she gave Grandpa's parents' names and his birthplace without too much trouble. "No, he wasn't

33

a member of anything. He just worked hard every day of his life and came home again. He was a good provider . . . me? Resurrection Lily Lutz Bridger." Having given her full name, Grandma then had to spell it before the questionnaire continued. "Just me and our granddaughter, Jamie Lee Bridger. No, no children." Grandma listened a moment, then repeated, "No children."

Kate and Jamie, eavesdropping, looked at each other and cringed. "That's logically and physically impossible," Jamie whispered to her friend.

"Agreed," Kate whispered back. "You can't have grandchildren but no children."

The woman on the other end of the phone must have been insisting the same thing, because Grandma's face changed. Jamie saw it coming and clutched at Kate's arm, frightened of that over-the-brink stare she had seen once before in those china-doll-blue eyes. Grandma stood very still, too still, too rigid. Out of her frozen face she shouted into the phone. Screamed, really. Not fumbling for words anymore. Even her voice had changed, going high and rapid and sure.

"No, he is survived by no children! No, he was preceded in death by no children! No sons! No daughters! No children! Just Jamie Lee, don't you understand? Yes, she is our granddaughter!"

Kate sat gaping. Jamie bolted to her feet and grabbed the phone out of her grandmother's hand. "Listen, we don't care what you put in the damn newspaper," she yelled into it, and she hung up.

Lily sagged and started to cry. Jamie put her arms

around her. "Never mind them," she said, forcing herself to speak softly.

"We couldn't have children!" Lily sobbed. "Daddy—didn't approve."

She could have been talking about her long-dead father or her dead husband. Jamie could not tell which and felt so stunned by fatigue and the craziness of everything that she did not care.

"Grandma," she whispered, "shhh. Here, sit down." She helped her grandmother to a chair beside Kate, who reached over to pat the old woman's hand.

"There's—nobody left—to take care—of me," Lily sobbed.

"Kate and I are going to take care of you," Jamie told her, and she meant it, yet how could they? Panic buzzed in the back of her mind, and her chest hurt with wanting something she might never have. *I'll try to take care of you—but who's gonna take care of me?*

In the middle of the night, Jamie got up to look for her grandfather's will.

Grandma lay sleeping. Sedated. She had not been able to stop crying, and Jamie had called the doctor even though it was Sunday, and the doctor had prescribed a tranquilizer. Kate's mother had picked it up at the pharmacy and put the cost on her charge card. So Grandma was okay for the time being, till morning. Grandma was sleeping, Kate was asleep amid a pile of quilts on the floor of Jamie's room, but Jamie could not sleep.

I'm the one who needs a tranquilizer, she thought. Just

joking. She did not want to ever be a pill-popping poor soul like her grandmother.

Barefoot, Jamie padded out of her bedroom. From the wall above her bed a white-tailed deer doe and fawn watched her with big scared charcoal eyes—they were her best work so far. Their frightened gaze seemed to follow her in the dark. To get to the stairs she had to walk through Grandpa's room—ick. She felt like he was lying there, not down in the basement of the funeral home.

But she made it through the room and down the dark stairs, because she had to. In the living room she took a deep breath and turned on the green glass banker's lamp by the rolltop desk where Grandpa kept his papers. Then she stood for a moment. The pool of light seemed tiny in the huge dark night, and Grandpa seemed to have followed her downstairs, seemed to lurk in the shadow of the recliner. Grandpa, who never let anybody near his things.

"He's dead," Jamie said aloud, and defiantly she opened the desk.

Pigeonholed ranks of papers faced her. She pulled them out a wad at a time, scanning them and then putting them back where she had found them. Grandpa had lined things up like soldiers: stamps and envelopes, rent receipts, car lease receipts—Jamie wondered, for such a controlling person, why did Grandpa rent a house rather than own one, lease a car rather than buy one? Now that he was dead, there wasn't even a house Grandma could really call her own, a car she could sell for spending money—not that it wouldn't have been in Grandpa's name anyway. Stupid, sticky old man with his life regimented into slots. Jamie searched through old utility bills, old tax bills, product warranties, Super Thrift and Wal-Mart receipts arranged by date, paycheck stubs. She was sitting in the desk chair studying the paycheck stubs when Kate came downstairs like a long-legged ghost in a big nightshirt.

"There you are!" Kate whispered. "Are you okay?"

"I'm fine," Jamie said, but she glowered at the paycheck stubs. "Look how much money he made, and she had to beg for every dollar she spent."

"Jamie, can't you look at that stuff tomorrow? Get some sleep."

"I don't want to upset Grandma." Jamie put the pay stubs back in their pigeonhole and opened the top drawer. "It would freak her out if she saw me doing this. He used to take care of everything. Paid the bills, did the banking, figured the taxes, and she would sign at the bottom." Jamie was sorting through the income-tax forms in the drawer. "He would cover the numbers with his hand so she wouldn't see."

"He didn't want her to see how much he made?" Kate exclaimed.

"That's what I've been trying to tell you! She doesn't know anything. She doesn't know if he had life insurance. She doesn't know if he had a safe-deposit box anywhere."

Kate folded herself into a surprisingly compact shape and sat on the carpeted floor, peering up. "Didn't she ever ask him about things like that?"

"I don't think so." Finished with the top drawer, Jamie shoved it closed and pulled out the next one. "Look at the way she is. He practically wiped her nose for her."

"But did he make her get that way, or was she always that way and did he just take care of her?"

"I don't know." Jamie blinked rapidly to clear her mind of the question. "Jeez, don't ask me stuff like that. You're giving me a headache." Really, it was Grandpa's desk that was giving Jamie a headache. All those papers. Bills to be paid, stacked in one corner. Deposit slips, canceled checks. Grandpa's spare checks, plain cheap ones of course, no pictures. A sheaf of beige-colored bank statements in the bottom drawer.

"The only thing she's sure of is that he made a will," Jamie said, "because she says he changed it to put me in it."

"Shouldn't your lawyer have a copy?"

Jamie stopped rooting through papers long enough to give Kate a look.

"Let me guess," Kate said. "She doesn't remember who your lawyer is."

"Bingo. You win the prize." Jamie turned back to her excavations. "The bank has a lawyer who's going to look at the will for us, if I can ever find the stupid—"

Her fingertips tapped against something. She lifted all the papers, and under them sat a flat metal box.

"Bingo," Kate said.

"Maybe." Jamie pulled the box out of the drawer and sat it in her lap. It was a heavy little thing, fireproof. The lid would not lift open for her.

"Locked."

"Where's the key? On his key ring?"

They tiptoed up to his bedroom together to retrieve the key ring from his dresser top. No luck—there was no little key that fit. Nor was it in the bottom of any of the desk drawers, or in one of the pigeonholes, or hanging on a wall anywhere.

"I am going down to the basement to find a hacksaw," grumbled Jamie, whose small supply of patience seemed to be all taken up by her grandmother. "Or a blowtorch."

"You'll fry the will or saw it in half," Kate protested. "There are people called locksmiths, you know."

"As if we have money to—"

"Oh, chill out." Kate was poking around in the desk. Her hand bumped against a section of ornamental woodwork between pigeonholes, and it moved. "Hey!" She pulled at it. A secret compartment slid open, and there lay a little key.

Jamie snatched it and tried it in the keyhole of the metal box. It fit. She turned it and opened the box.

"You're welcome," Kate told her sweetly.

"Uh, thanks." There were only a few documents in the box, each in some sort of envelope. Jamie flipped through them: Grandpa's contract with his employer, Grandma and Grandpa's marriage record, a squarish brown envelope marked Birth Certificates.

Jamie froze with it in her hand. Suddenly she was not just looking for her grandfather's will any longer. Suddenly she was looking for herself.

"Open it," Kate urged softly.

"Please," Jamie whispered to the envelope as she pulled out the papers inside. Then she groaned. There was her birth certificate all right, along with Grandma's and Grandpa's. But it told her nothing. She saw only some numbers and her name, birthdate, and place of birth.

"Chicago?" Kate exclaimed, looking over her shoulder. "Is that where you lived before?"

"No. It wasn't a city." Jamie felt sure it had been a little town, almost country. Hadn't there been chickens in the backyard? She thought she remembered chickens—but the memories seemed as faded as old photos, and she felt suddenly very tired. "Damn. I thought they put your parents' names on birth certificates."

"Looks like they don't."

"Looks like." Jamie returned the papers to their envelope and reached for the next one.

It was the will.

Kind of lightweight, as wills go. Simple, only two pages long. Jamie pulled it out of its envelope and glanced at the first few paragraphs, having no idea how important this document would turn out to be to her. Much as she expected, it left everything to Grandma, and the lawyer would figure out the technicalities in the morning. Good, one less thing for Grandma to worry about. *God, I could sleep now.* Dog tired. Dopey tired. She slipped the will back into its envelope—

And jumped as if she had been cattle-prodded. "You idiot!" she cried at herself.

"Huh?" At Jamie's sudden yell Kate jumped too.

"I almost missed it! Look!" Jamie jabbed her finger at the will. Not the will, really, but the envelope it was in.

It was the original envelope that had brought it in the mail. Imprinted in the upper left-hand corner was the return address: "S. J. Lampeterson, Attorney at Law, 160 Market Street, Silver Valley, Pennsylvania." Typed below was the mailing address: "Mr. Cletus Uru Bridger, 35 Sweet Gum Lane, Silver Valley, PA."

"That's where I'm from," said Jamie, her voice shaking. "It's where I come from. Silver Valley. That's where my parents might be."

Chapter

"Grandma, please eat something," Jamie begged. Days after the funeral there was still food left over from when Grandpa had died. Jamie had warmed up somebody's homemade chicken pot pie, and her grandmother was sitting at the table with her, watching her eat it. Grandma had stopped crying all the time and seemed calm these days—quite calm—but was not eating.

"I can't, dear. Once that's gone, we don't have anything."

"Grandma, we have plenty. The insurance check came." Jamie spoke words worn down from having been said many times. Grandpa had provided for Grandma with life insurance after all. Jamie had found the policy in the metal box right under the will. So there was insurance money for Grandma to live on, and besides that there was plenty of money in the bank, what with all of Grandpa's years of penny-pinching. Once the will was probated, that money would all be Grandma's too. But she did not seem to understand any of this. To Grandma, unless Grandpa brought home a paycheck and took her to the Super Thrift to convert it into groceries, food did not exist in the universe as she knew it.

Jamie tried again. "Have some soup at least."

"No, thank you, honey. You go ahead and eat."

There was a tap at the door, and Kate came in with a fistful of papers. She had been coming over every day after school to bring Jamie's assignments and explain what had been done in civics, German, algebra. The two of them were hoping to get Jamie through what little was left of the school year that way. Jamie had tried going to school one day, and had come home to find Grandma sitting on the floor under the kitchen table. Just sitting there.

Kate set the papers on the table and hugged Grandma around the shoulders. "Hello, sweetie," Grandma told her.

"Have some pot pie?" Jamie offered it to Kate.

"Sure." The Bridgers ate early, or at least the one Bridger who was eating did. The Garibays ate late, and Kate was skinny as a rake; she could handle two suppers. "Everybody says hi," she told Jamie as she got herself a plate. "Doosie is on crutches again. Fell down the stairs."

Jamie grinned. For no particular reason Doosie had been falling down stairs about once every three months since Jamie had known her.

"Bert the Pervert chewed a whole package of cinnamon gum at once without taking the wrappers off. He says the paper tastes better than the gum."

"Some people would burn their hair to get attention," Jamie said.

"That's Bert." Kate sat down and cheerfully went on with her report. "Bethany got mad at her father and she's missed the bus every day this week. She hides out in the bathroom until after her bus is announced, just to make him come pick her up."

"Jeez." Jamie was impressed. "I can't imagine ever doing that."

"You're such a good girl," Kate said wickedly.

Unable to retort as she would have liked because Grandma was there, Jamie gave her a look.

Kate smiled. "Well, anyway, everybody says to tell you they miss you."

"Tell them I miss them too." This was all too true. Jamie's friends phoned now and then, but she had not seen them since she had been staying home from school, because she did not feel as if she could invite them over to her house, the way Grandma was. What would Grandma do if people came in? Cry? Stare? Smile? Bake cookies? Crawl under the table again?

Kate helped herself to pot pie. "Aren't you eating, Mamaw?" she asked Mrs. Bridger, though she already knew the answer.

"I'm not feeling very hungry right now, honey. You eat."

Kate eyed Grandma thoughtfully as she did so. She and Jamie had talked about Grandma, trying to think of ways to get her started eating again.

"Mamaw, I saw Mrs. Leweski down the street today," Kate told Grandma earnestly. "She says to let you know she'll drive you to the store or anywhere you have to go, to run errands or whatever. She says she'll be glad to."

Kate's theory was, if Grandma felt better about life, maybe she would eat.

Grandma nodded politely but barely seemed to hear. "I think I'll go upstairs now," she murmured. "You two enjoy your meal." She wavered up from her chair and shuffled out of the room.

Jamie and Kate set down their forks and just looked at each other, listening to Grandma tread slowly up the stairs.

"Did she eat anything today at all?" Kate whispered when Grandma was far enough away.

"Tea with sugar."

"Nothing else? Not even noodle soup?"

Jamie shook her head. She knew too that Grandma could not go on like this. Already the big bones were showing white in her wrists. What if she got weak and fell? What if she fainted from starving herself?

"Are you thinking of getting her to a doctor?" Kate asked, reading Jamie's mind, as usual.

Jamie said slowly, "She's already on pills. A doctor would probably put her in a hospital, and can you see her? She's hardly been out of this house since I can remember. A hospital would freak her out so bad she would just lie there and die."

"She wouldn't really. They would feed her with tubes."

"Then she would just lie there and exist."

"That's kind of what she does anyway."

Like a doormat. Lying there. Just taking it and taking it, taking whatever steps on her.

Her own anger surprised Jamie like a scarlet tornado

45

out of nowhere. "Shut up!" she hissed at Kate. The storm inside her blasted her to her feet. She bumped her plate, spilling pot pie across the table. Saw Kate goggling at her. Bolted out the door before the snarl on her face could turn to bite, before she could say anything worse to her friend. Stood in her yard panting, gulping in deep breaths of the cool night air to calm down.

She badly needed a walk in the woods. Getting out in the country, being with nature, sitting with her sketch pad under a tree, maybe seeing a deer, a grouse, a red squirrel—that was what Jamie lived for. But no way could she do it anymore, with Grandma needing her.

The best she could do was to look at the sky. The sun had set, and floating in the magenta afterglow were a thin silver arc of new moon and a single bright star.

Jamie gazed, breathing more steadily now. The moon was her mother, the star her father. Far, far away.

The kitchen door let out a rectangle of yellow light, then closed again. Kate came and stood beside Jamie. "What'd I say?" she asked softly.

Jamie turned and hugged Kate around the neck, resting her head on Kate's shoulder.

"You okay?" Kate's hands came up and patted her back.

Jamie lifted her head to look into Kate's face. "You're going to think I'm crazy," she said, "but can you help me anyway? I just realized what I've got to do."

Days before, the first minute she got a chance, Jamie had tried calling the lawyer Lampeterson, the one whose name was on the envelope of Grandpa's will. No go—he

46

was not there in Silver Valley anymore. It had seemed like a dead end. Forget finding parents a while. There had been a funeral to arrange and attend, and Grandma to think of.

But now, thinking of Grandma, Jamie saw a chance thin and shining as a new moon. Knowing what to do, she also knew she had to do it soon, before things got even worse.

She told Kate. Kate told her she was crazy. Jamie knew she had to do it anyway.

That night, after Grandma was in bed, Jamie found the new checkbook—still the plain yellow "safety" kind, no pictures. Jamie made a mental note that when she grew up she was going to have pretty checks with rainbows and sunrises. Meanwhile, she wrecked only one check before she succeeded in writing one out to "Cash."

In the morning she got Grandma to sign it. Then she took a quick bike ride into Dexter, visited the bank, and picked up a bus schedule at the Pharm-All. Back home she packed a tote bag: a packet of graham crackers, two apples, two bananas, a change of underwear. That afternoon she watched for Kate to get home from school. The minute Kate appeared, Jamie headed for the Garibay place.

"You're crazy," Kate told her for the tenth time, eating cheese curls with a resigned expression. She pushed the bag toward Jamie.

Jamie shook her head and pushed it back. "So did you ask your mother for permission?"

"Yes, it's okay. Don't worry about Mamaw. Just take care of yourself, all right? Did you get money?"

"Yup."

"Well, don't lose it. Or, I mean, lose it if you have to, but don't let anybody hurt you. If you get in any kind of trouble, call me at your place, or you can call here and Mom will leave the answering machine on, or—"

"Kate, it's not like I'm going to New York City!"

"I still wish somebody was going with you. Where are you going to stay?"

"Kate, I'll handle it!"

Kate had told her parents only that Jamie was going back where she used to live for a visit.

Jamie had not told Grandma a thing so far, and Grandma had not asked a thing, not even what the check was for.

Grandma ate one saltine, nothing more, at supper.

I have to tell her, Jamie was thinking. *I can't put it off any longer.* Yet she carried her dishes to the sink without saying anything.

Almost whispering, Grandma said, "Jamie, I wonder if you would fix my hair for me."

"Sure."

"It seems like such a bother for me to do it myself anymore," Grandma apologized. Her voice, which had never been strong, seemed to have gotten weaker since Grandpa died.

Grandma stayed where she was, sitting in the kitchen chair, and Jamie stood behind her. When Jamie carefully pulled the hairpins out and undid Grandma's braids, Grandma's hair rippled over the back of the chair clear to the floor, a reverse waterfall, white at the top, brown

48

at the bottom. Grandma's hair was wonderful, so thick, but her face seemed pulled taut by its weight, and thin, and lily pale.

Brushing her grandmother's hair with the natural bristle brush, making sure she gave it long careful strokes clear to the ends, Jamie thought how different Grandma seemed. Frail. I'm the one taking care of her now, she thought. When Grandma's hair was all brushed smooth, Jamie plaited it in two Heidi braids that tapered so fine they ended in points, like knitting needles. She coiled the braids like a crown on her grandmother's head and pinned them in place. Then quietly, without having to dither about it anymore, she said, "Grandma, I have to go away for a couple of days."

Grandma just nodded. Did not even ask why, or where. Jamie wondered if she had really heard or understood.

"Katie is going to stay with you." Jamie bent to look straight into Lily's bewildered blue eyes, trying to see whether she comprehended. "She'll be here with you the whole time. Today's Friday. She'll be here when you wake up tomorrow morning, Saturday, and I'll be gone. But I'll be back Sunday night." Kate had to go to school on Monday.

"All right, dear." It was as if Grandma were saying, "All right, Daddy." Jamie's heart ached.

I have to find somebody to help. Somebody has to know whether she has relatives, a brother, a sister, a son, a daughter—my father or mother . . .

Kate came and stayed overnight. Before dawn the next

morning Jamie was on a Greyhound headed toward Silver Valley.

It was not very far away, three hours, and it was in the same state, but coming down out of the mountains, leaving the wooded ridges and coal slag heaps behind, Jamie felt as if she were traveling to a different country. In the green rolling farmland to the east it was summer instead of spring. The roads were crowded with more traffic than Jamie had ever seen. There were shopping malls outside of towns. People looked different. Groomed. Stylish. Sophisticated.

Jamie rode with her stomach knotted. Her straight hair and bangs felt as old-fashioned as Grandma's braids. She had a button-up sweater instead of a jacket. Her jeans were baggy. *I can't believe I'm doing this. They aren't going to want to talk with me.*

I am going to be sick if I don't get out of this bus soon.

"Silver Valley," the driver roared in a bored voice.

Jamie's stomach lurched, and she peered out her window. It was a beautiful town. Larkspur and daylilies grew along fences. Pink and crimson rambling roses climbed on porches. Jamie saw white paint, bright glass, wreaths on doors. It was a town made for sunshine.

Why did they ever leave here?

She got off the bus and stood on the sidewalk, thinking. How could she find Mr. Lampeterson, the lawyer? She already knew his name was not in the phone book. Dead end; try another route. If she could find the house she remembered . . . something might happen.

" 'Scuse me," she asked a woman planting petunias in

a window box, "can you tell me where Sweet Gum Lane is?"

Twenty minutes later she rounded the corner and stopped, a strange feeling beating like wings in her chest. There was no landmark she could consciously recognize, yet she knew she had been there before.

She walked slowly, looking for the address, but knew the house before she saw the number. There it was. Small—had it always been so small? But somebody loved it. The gingerbread on the porch was painted wild-rose pink and periwinkle blue and buttercup yellow as well as white.

Jamie walked up to the house. Yes, there was a half-circle of glass, a fanlight, over the front door. She felt too shaky to ring the doorbell, stood there a minute, then walked around the side to the backyard, staring. The yard was still fenced with chicken wire—she had remembered that right. There was a big Japanese maple—hadn't she played under it, hadn't she climbed in the low branches? Where was the swing set? She knew there had been a swing set.

"Hello," a pleasant voice called.

Jamie jumped. Intent on the yard, she had not noticed the woman sitting on the back steps. "Hi," she replied, but her voice was not behaving. It came out a whisper.

The woman put down whatever she had been doing, stood up, and walked over to face Jamie across the low wire-mesh fence. "You look kind of lost, honey," she remarked. "Something wrong?"

"Not exactly . . ." Then Jamie blurted it out. "I think I used to live here when I was little."

"Really?" The woman's homely face lit up in a smile. There were deep lines in her cheeks and laugh crinkles around her eyes. Blinking, Jamie realized this woman might have been as old as Grandma, judging by her skin. It was the way she wore blue jeans instead of a housedress, Jamie decided, that made her seem younger. Or maybe her sandy-colored hair, so tousled Jamie had not noticed it was dusted with gray. Or maybe her smile.

"What's your name?" the woman wanted to know.

"Jamie Bridger."

"Bridger! That sounds about right. I believe the Bridgers were the people before the people before me." With sudden, startling ease the woman vaulted her fence to stand beside Jamie. "Well, then, you'd better have a look around, hadn't you?" she invited happily. "Come on!" She led Jamie alongside the house to the front porch and in the front door.

The house took in Jamie like an embrace. A dozen memories rushed back at once. "Oh!" Jamie cried. "The light, I remember the light!" The old crystal-and-aluminum ceiling fixture was the same, centered amid decorative plasterwork. "And the swirlies on the ceiling! I used to lie there . . ." Yes, the window seat was still there. "I used to lie stretched out on that, I was so little, and just look up. And the wallpaper!" Still with the same fat white sheep grazing by the same blue curlicue bushes. "Look what I used to do." Jamie ran to a corner, and there, up to a height of about three feet, the paper was damaged. "I used to take my thumbnail and do that." Jamie stood staring at the tiny crescent-shaped perforations following the corner up to where she had not been able to reach any higher. Now that she was taller than her grandmother, it was hard to believe she had ever been so small.

The woman who owned the house stood broadly smiling. "I guess I'm not much of a home decorator," she drawled. The place was comfortably junked up. "That wallpaper's been there that long?"

"Yes. Mama put it up." Jamie blinked. "Grandma, I mean." Jamie giggled. "She was mad when she noticed the corners."

"I bet. Sometimes I want to take a bunch of crayons and color the sheep. You think I should?"

Jamie burst out laughing. It was just what she had always wanted to do when she lived there.

"You want to see your bedroom?"

"Oh! Yes, thank you, um—"

"Shirley."

Jamie hesitated, not used to calling adults by their first names.

"Shirley Dubbs. As in rub-a-dub Dubbs, three men need three tubs. Something like that." This woman seemed a little bit weird, but nice. She led the way upstairs. "Okay, which one was yours?"

"The—little one up front, with the—dormers. . . ."

Jamie stood staring at light streaming in on a white-painted bed under a puffy quilt, a fuzzy rug on the floor.

"I don't use the upstairs much," Shirley said.

The room seemed not used at all, not even for junk. It looked like it was suspended in time, waiting for her. There were pillows in white pillowcases on the bed. There was a white linen cloth with a tatted border on the dresser top. The peach-colored quilt on the bed matched the flocked wallpaper—Jamie's wallpaper. She remembered it.

"I took the bunny decals off the door," Shirley said. "Sorry. If I'd known you were coming, I would have left them."

"That's okay," Jamie whispered.

"You came back to visit friends, Jamie?"

"Sort of." Jamie made herself stop staring at the bedroom. "I'm sort of trying to track down a few things. Do you remember my family at all?"

"Not a bit. I'm not from around here."

"Are the neighbors the same ones? I mean, you know, have any of them been here long?"

Shirley was getting a small, worried frown. "Most of them haven't been here as long as I have."

"Oh."

"Something wrong, Jamie?"

"Um, no." Jamie did not have the heart to ask her if she knew a lawyer named Lampeterson. "I'd better go. Thank you for letting me look around, Mrs., uh, Miss—"

"Shirley."

"Um, Shirley, thanks, I really appreciate it." Jamie hurried downstairs and out the door. As she jogged down Sweet Gum Lane, she glanced back once at the house. Shirley was standing on its gingerbreaded porch, looking after her.

Chapter

5

Kate was not much of a morning person. She barely stirred when Jamie headed out to bike to the bus station—just mumbled something like, "Good luck," and went back to sleep. But around eight that Saturday morning she woke up and forced herself to keep her eyes open, knowing she had to get up pretty soon to take care of Mamaw.

Poor Mamaw. Kate hated seeing her so flattened. Kate remembered when she and Jamie were little kids running in the backyard summer dusk; Mamaw would come out and bring them peanut-butter cookies and admire how many lightning bugs they had caught. She remembered Mamaw would help them both dress up for Halloween, and give them coffee (mostly milk) when they came back with bags of loot, and let them sit at the table talking late, like grown-ups. If Jamie were giving Mamaw away, even as badly as things were going, Kate would have taken her. It would have been nice to have a grandma, and Mrs.

Bridger was the best, and Kate had always felt that way. She had called Mrs. Bridger "Mamaw" since she had known her.

At only ten past eight, far earlier than her usual Saturday sleep-in time, Kate groaned and got herself up and moving.

Poor Mamaw. Poor Jamie. Kate went to brush her teeth, feeling heavy with a leaden sense of what she had not yet told Jamie, not at such a bad time. What a time for Dad to decide he needed to look for a new job, and for Mom to go to work for the state. What a time for the Garibays to decide they had to move.

As if any time would be a good time. Kate still could not believe she really had to do this. Leave Jamie behind. Leave her friends, and the home she had lived in all her life.

Kate did not hear Mamaw stirring anywhere around the house. Probably the pills were making her sleepy, and she was still in bed. That was okay, if she would just eat.

Dressed in T-shirt and jeans and sneakers, Kate tiptoed to peek into Lily's bedroom. *Maybe if Mamaw's awake, I'll bring her breakfast in bed.*

But the bed was empty. It did not look as if it had been slept in. Or maybe it was made already.

"Huh!" Kate headed downstairs. Mamaw must have gotten up early, must be down in the kitchen after all.

No. There was no sign of her.

Kate ran back upstairs. Had Mamaw slipped past her while she was in the bathroom? Was Mamaw in the other bedroom, the one with its shades pulled down, the one

Mr. Bridger had slept in? Kate hated going into that room, and pushed the door open gingerly. "Mamaw?" she whispered, feeling like an intruder. What if the old woman was in there crying?

But there was no one. Nothing but the shadows.

"Where the—" Starting to get scared, Kate ran downstairs again and lunged out the back door to check the yard. She knew she was grasping at straws. Even when she was feeling okay, Mamaw seldom went out of the house.

She was not out there. Kate ran all the way around the house to be sure.

Back inside she stood puffing and panicked. "Mamaw!" she shouted to the house. "Mrs. Bridger! Mamaw!"

Nothing. The place was as still as death.

No. No, she couldn't have killed herself; she wouldn't have done that.

But where was she? What was left to check? The basement. Kate darted down there. Nothing. The attic? It was reached by a trapdoor that Mamaw was probably too big to fit through. Even as a younger, less cushy person, Mamaw had been scared to climb up there on the ladder. Besides, Kate would have seen the ladder standing in the hallway.

What would Mamaw have done, the way she was feeling? With Jamie gone? Where would she be?

"Think," Kate whispered to herself, standing by the kitchen table, pressing her hands to her head. One more minute of this and she would have to call her parents, or the cops, or both. "Think, Kate Marie Garibay. *Think.*"

The kitchen table. Kate could see under it; there was nothing there, but—Mamaw had hidden under the kitchen table when Jamie went to school.

She was hiding.

Kate ran upstairs to Lily's bedroom, then stopped. Took a deep breath and told herself to be quiet and calm. Walked across the room and gently opened the closet door.

It was an old-fashioned walk-in closet, deep, built big enough to be a baby's nursery in a pinch, with a ledge around the sides so shoes and junk wouldn't collect on the floor. Plenty of room in there for a frightened old woman to hide.

"Oh, Mamaw!" Kate kept her voice steady, but her knees wobbled. She sank down to sit beside the old woman huddled on the floor under a row of flowered cotton housedresses. "Are you all right?" She gathered Lily into a hug. "I was scared. Are you scared?"

"No, sweetie, I'm fine." Mamaw slumped slack in her arms but spoke with desperate dignity. "I just—I felt as though I might float away, that was all."

"Didn't you sleep at all?"

"I slept some. Hard surfaces are good for the back. I think I slept very well. I must have. I heard you calling, dear, but Daddy did not want me to answer you."

Kate opened her mouth, then closed it again. Better not touch that. "Well, I was going to bring you breakfast in bed," she said too cheerfully after a moment. "I guess I'll bring it right here."

"No, thank you, dear. I am not at all hungry."

But Mamaw had to eat! Kate's thoughts raced—

maybe if she could get Mamaw into the kitchen? "Would you like to come down and watch me eat?"

"Not today, honey. I believe I am going to stay in here for the time being. The light is hard on my eyes."

Kate leaned back against the closet wall and closed her own eyes. It was going to be a long weekend.

The address Jamie had for Attorney Lampeterson was occupied by another lawyer, or rather lawyers: G. Pettijohn, A. Fox, and Ian L. Russell, Attorneys at Law. The sign did not indicate Saturday office hours, but Jamie pushed at the door anyway. There were no Bridgers in the phone book for her to call—it was not a common name. She had looked in the yellow pages, trying to figure out where Grandpa used to work, without luck. Now she could not think what else to do except come here.

The door swung open. Somebody was working.

Jamie stepped into an unlit reception room. A youngish man in wire-rimmed glasses, padding across the thick carpet with an armload of files, stopped to peer at her. "May I help you?"

Jamie felt like an idiot, but said it. "I need to find Attorney Lampeterson."

"He's retired and moved to Florida."

At least he was still alive. "Do you, uh, by any chance have his address?"

"His daughter does." The man turned away and shouted, "Hey, Ian! Somebody to see you!"

Ian?

Ian L. Russell, Attorney at Law. Ian Lampeterson Russell, hometown girl. This was her office now.

"Who is it?" Ian's voice floated back from somewhere in the rear of the building. She sounded annoyed, and the wire-rimmed man grinned.

"She gets cranky when she has to work on Saturdays," he explained to Jamie. "What's your name?" She told him. "Jamie Bridger!" he yelled to Ian.

Ian did not yell back. Instead, quick footsteps sounded and there she was, a tall, redheaded woman, somehow dressed for success even in jeans, attractive, almost as gorgeous as Kate. She came rushing out, but when she saw Jamie she stopped short, looking astonished.

"But—but you're a girl!" she blurted.

It occurred to Jamie that a woman named Ian should not be so astounded to see a girl named Jamie.

"And you're young!"

Being young was not so amazing either. What was the matter with this woman? Jamie stared. The wire-rimmed guy was staring. Ian felt the stares and blushed.

"I'm sorry, I'm being rude. I—I thought you were the Jamie Bridger I went to high school with."

Jamie's heart started pounding so hard it shoved her a step forward. Her hand stretched out. She wanted to shout questions, but her jaw seemed to have disconnected from her brain, and her mouth wouldn't work.

"Are you sure you're not him?" Ian still looked boggled. "You look just like him."

It had to be, it had to be, it had to be! She was named after him.

With a fierce effort Jamie got her mouth working. "Where is he now?" she whispered.

"I don't know. I wish I did. I'm on the class reunion committee, and he's one of the people we'd really like to find." Ian looked hard at Jamie. "Hey, you're white as a ghost. Sit down." She steered Jamie into an armchair and held her there by the shoulders. "Andy, get her some water!"

Wire rims hurried off.

"Take a deep breath," Ian instructed.

Jamie did, but let it out in a rush of words. "Tell me about him," she begged. "Please, just tell me anything you know about him. I'm looking for him. I think he might be my father."

Jamie ran down Market Street, her tote bag bouncing, hurrying to get to the Silver Valley Public Library. According to Ian, she had less than half an hour before closing time.

She ran up the stairs to the reference desk. Twenty minutes till closing.

"Yes?"

"Is this where you keep the old high-school yearbooks?"

A few minutes later, her hands shaking as she turned the glossy pages, Jamie found the other Jamie Bridger's tiny black-and-white pictured face.

He looked just like her.

It was like seeing herself in some sort of time-machine mirror. It was weird and frightening and break-my-heart beautiful and take-my-breath-away strange. Jamie stared for minutes, and the other Jamie Bridger stared soberly back at her across the distance of the years, and everything Ian had told her about him floated like butterflies through her mind.

"He didn't graduate. In the middle of junior year he disappeared."

"He was sweet. I had the worst crush on him."

"He was genuinely nice. I mean, a lot of people act nice, but Jamie really was nice. Back then it seemed like most of the boys were oinks, but Jamie treated girls like human beings."

"I never knew Jamie had a girlfriend. I didn't think he was allowed to date."

"I guess there was a lot I didn't know. I'm one of those people—I'm always the last one who knows anything." Rueful laugh. "Obviously he must have had somebody, because here you are. But I still just can't believe it. I can't see Jamie getting a girl pregnant."

"I never heard about any baby. They must have kept you in the house, kiddo."

"Yes, they lived out there on Sweet Gum Lane. That was one strange family. I'm sorry, Jamie, I shouldn't be talking about your grandparents this way, but it's the truth. He was the nicest boy, and they threw him out with the garbage."

"No, no brothers or sisters. He was an only child."

"I walked up to Mr. Bridger once and asked him if he heard from Jamie, and he said to me, 'Jamie is dead,' with this look that gave me the chills. To him, his son was dead."

"He just disappeared. Never finished school. Nobody seems to know where he went."

Looking at the yearbooks, Jamie double-checked her mental math. Yes, the dates seemed about right. The boy named Jamie had left Silver Valley the winter of his junior year. The next fall, baby Jamie had come along.

She, Jamie, must have been what he had done that was so awful it made Grandpa disown him. Jamie felt queasy thinking it, that she was the reason he had been kicked out in the cold.

Ian's nice. I think she really, really liked him.

Ian had spent half the afternoon talking with Jamie, trying to help her figure things out. Ian had even phoned her father, the retired lawyer, in Florida. Once he understood the situation, Attorney Lampeterson had confirmed what Jamie and Ian had suspected: Mr. Bridger had changed his will in order to cut his son Jamie out of it. Yes, there was a baby the Bridgers had kept under wraps. A few years later the Bridgers had left town and dropped out of sight.

They were ashamed of me.

Jamie had been back once looking for his parents, Attorney Lampeterson said. While Ian was in law school. Hadn't he mentioned it to her? Sorry, dear. No, he didn't know where the young man was now.

Did he know about me? Did he come back to take me with him?

There were two more pictures of Jamie Bridger in the yearbooks, his sophomore-year photo and his freshman-year photo, looking very young and shy. He seemed to

have had a hard time smiling. He had not been in any
activities or played on any teams. Probably Daddy had
not approved.

Just like he didn't approve of me.

There was a tired feeling in Jamie that she recognized
from longtime experience: It was anger she could not do
anything about.

There's one thing I can do. I am going to find him.

She got photocopies of the yearbook pages, enlarged
to show Jamie's face better, and then she had to leave.
The library was closing.

Standing on the sidewalk in front of it, she realized
she felt weak with hunger. She had been so jittery all day,
she had not eaten, and now it was late. The sun was low.
There did not seem to be a McDonald's or a motel in
Silver Valley. Okay, Jamie told herself, she could survive
on graham crackers and apples if she had to. But night
was coming, and she did not have any idea where she was
going to stay.

Chapter

6

"Um, Ms. Dubbs? Hi, this is Jamie, you know, I was there this afternoon?"

"Shirley." The woman's voice carried forcefully over the phone line. "Call me Shirley. Of course I know who you are. What can I do for you, Jamie?"

Jamie had already asked people on the street and in the drugstore whether there was a tourist home or a bed-and-breakfast where she could stay. Nobody knew of any. People had looked at her strangely. At the pay phone she had called Ian's office number—no answer, and no home number listed in the book. No motels or hotels with Silver Valley addresses were in the yellow pages, either. Calling this woman who lived in what used to be Jamie's house was a last resort, and Jamie knew it. She felt pathetic doing it, like a little lost kid—couldn't keep her voice from quivering.

"I was wondering. I, uh, I'm looking for a place to stay—"

"And you want the spare bedroom? Sure, no problem, Jamie."

Really she had been going to ask Shirley to give her a ride to a motel somewhere. Shirley's offer caught her by happy surprise, and she started to stammer. "I—I'll pay you—"

"To stay in your own room? You don't have to pay me, Jamie. Just come on out."

You barely know her, Jamie reminded herself after she hung up the phone. *Be careful.* Yet walking out to the little house on Sweet Gum Lane felt like going home.

Shirley was waiting at the door. She had a funny face, steepled eyebrows over round bright eyes, a pointed chin, teeth fit to drive an orthodontist crazy. "Hungry?" she asked.

Oh, good grief. Jamie decided to leave some money under the pillow if Shirley wouldn't accept it any other way. "I, uh—"

"Of course you're hungry. Come on, dinner's on the table."

Dinner was bits and pieces thrown together: some take-out Chinese fried rice, a couple of barbecued chicken wings, red grapes, Pepsi, a deviled egg, a kiwifruit, Irish soda bread, carrot sticks, butter-almond ice cream. It was good, especially once some items got help from the microwave, but it was not like any meal Grandma would ever have fixed. Grandma was just not the microwave type.

"How old are you, Jamie?" Shirley wanted to know as they were eating. "Sixteen?"

"Fourteen. Almost fifteen." Well, in five months.

"Jailbait. And you're here in big bad Silver Valley all by yourself?

Jamie nodded.

"Anybody you need to phone? Anybody worrying about you?"

Was Grandma worrying? Jamie thought about it, then shook her head. If anything, she was worrying about Grandma.

Shirley sighed, then tried the direct approach. "You mind telling me what's going on?"

Why not? Jamie told her. Telling Shirley everything she knew so far helped her sort it all out. Shirley's round eyes got more and more thoughtful as Jamie ate and talked.

"Huh," Shirley said. "Well, you could contact the courthouse of the county where you were born. Those numbers on your birth certificate go to a file where the long form is kept. See, what you've got is the short form. Somebody can find the file and look at the long form and tell you who it says your parents are."

For a moment Jamie felt furiously stupid. As if sensing this, Shirley got up to bring the ice cream.

"Um, yeah," Jamie said in a small voice. "I'll do that. But, like, I already know who my father is, and how do I find him?" As usual, she found herself more interested in her father than in her mother. Especially now that she knew his name. Jamie Bridger. Like hers.

"Huh," Shirley said thoughtfully again, handing Jamie her bowl of butter almond. "Well, pretty much the way you've been doing. As I was gathering my wits to tell you before you kited off this morning, kiddo, there is one old couple across the street, Mr. and Mrs. Wolgemuth, who've lived here longer than me. Maybe they might remember something. They go to bed kind of early," Shirley added as Jamie jumped up. "You can talk to them tomorrow."

Jamie went to bed kind of early herself, after helping with the dishes and watching a little TV. It had been a day as long and crowded as Shirley's teeth. Jamie knew so much more than she had known twelve hours before that her head felt leaky.

It was leaky. She was crying.

Lying there, gazing at the streetlamp patterns on the walls just the way a very small girl used to do, Jamie felt the tears running soundlessly down her temples into her hair. Where was that little kid now? Who was she really? Had anybody—did anybody—want her?

Dry up, Jamie told herself, looking around, feeling a need to blow her nose. *Damn, there's no Kleenex. Dry up, Jamie. Why are you crying when it's coming together?*

The house seemed to want her. The bedroom felt glad to have her back. Jamie turned her pillow over and went to sleep. Usually she slept badly in a strange bed, a strange place, but in this place she slept soundly till morning.

A sunny May morning. Jamie woke up feeling better than she had since Grandpa died. Ten minutes later she was downstairs throwing together some breakfast with Shirley. She liked the way Shirley explored the refrigerator like an unknown country, and the way Shirley used mismatched flea-market china. And the way a plush, oversized stuffed cow sat in its own chair at Shirley's table. There seemed to be a lot to like about Shirley.

Jamie ate apple slices dipped in honey and some corn muffins. "Good muffins," she told Shirley.

"Thank you. I bought them at Safeway all by myself."

"Do you think those people are up yet?"

"Wolgemuths? They'll be getting ready for church. Around noon would be the best time for you to catch them. You finished eating?" At Jamie's nod, Shirley got up, leaving the breakfast dishes on the table. She took two corn muffins in one hand and some apple slices in the other. "Why don't you come on out in the yard and meet the gang?" She opened the screen door with her rump.

The gang?

Jamie followed Shirley out to the big, fenced yard, where the grass, she noticed, grew long and shaggy and seemed dug up in spots, as if a little ghost girl had been making mud pies.

"Breakfast!" Shirley shouted. She pulled a wooden spoon out of the crotch of a maple tree and used it to beat on a big old turkey roaster hanging from a branch. WHANGG, WHANGG, WHANGGG. When the vibrations seemed to shake the world, Shirley stopped whanging and waited a moment. Nothing happened. "C'mon, breakfast!" Shirley hollered, and she beat on the roaster again.

Very slowly, the grass started to move.

Shirley put the spoon back and sat down on the ground under the tree. "Pull up a piece of backyard," she invited Jamie. "This is going to take a while."

Jamie sat, mouth open, watching. Something-or-others were creeping at her from all different directions.

"C'mon Toby, Burp, Lola!" Shirley yelled. "They

can't really hear me," she said more quietly to Jamie. "I just like to make noise. Somebody has to shake up this neighborhood." She bellowed, "C'mon, Bink, Lou, Cher, Poo! Suzy, Wink, get the lead out! Breakfast!"

A thumb-shaped, yellow polka-dot head parted the grass near Jamie. She flinched—for a moment she thought it was a snake. Then she saw a wrinkled, clawed foot. The foot scrabbled and strained, heaving a yellow-and-brown high-domed shell an inch closer to Shirley.

"Turtles!"

"Just sit real still, and they won't mind you. Well, good morning, Bobo!" Shirley offered the nearest turtle a bit of apple. "Hungry?"

"Box turtles," Jamie amended. "Big old box turtles. The whole yard is full of them!" She saw grass moving everywhere.

"There's twenty-one of them right now. Every time I see one trying to get itself mushed on the road, I bring it home. Whoa, they're really motoring. Just look at 'em tearing up here for their goodies." Several of the lumbering land tortoises were now visible, and Shirley eyed them with a fond smile. "Good morning, Otto. Good morning, Mimi."

"How can you tell—oh, I see!" The names were painted on top of the shells, calligraphed there in small, elegant red and bright-green and enamel-blue letters. Mimi had a border of little pink hearts running around her shell as well. "You, uh, you label them."

"And customize them a bit sometimes. I try not to interfere with their natural beauty." Shirley said this with a straight face, feeding Bobo (he had finally crossed the

70

remaining three feet to reach her) a tiny wedge of apple from her hand.

"May I pick one up?"

"By all means. Take Bobo away before he gets fat."

Jamie lifted the box turtle. From the heft of him, he was fat already. Being handled by a stranger, he pulled himself into his shell. The hinged part of his plastron closed with a hissing sound.

"Sit him in your lap and he'll come out eventually," Shirley said.

Jamie cradled Bobo, so full of questions that she had actually forgotten about Grandma and all the rest of it for the moment. "How do you name them?"

"Short, to fit on the shell."

"I mean, how do you know which ones are girls and which ones are boys?"

Shirley tilted her head toward two turtles not far away. "That's how."

Jamie looked. One of the turtles was trying to crawl on top of the other. "Oh!" Jamie felt herself turn pink.

"What can I say? It's spring." Shirley grinned toothily.

"Oh." Jamie tried to think of something sensible to say but only succeeded in blurting out, "So they're going to have babies?"

Shirley peered at the turtles involved, then smiled more gently. "Not them. Okay, really how I tell is the males have red eyes. And what we got there is Sam and Burp. Two males."

Jamie felt her blush progress from pink to a shade so hot it felt like fuchsia.

"I am embarrassing the heck out of you," Shirley said,

concerned. "I don't mean to. Don't matter to me if the boys play with the boys sometimes, and the girls with the girls. It's natural."

"It is?" Jamie had heard most of the usual jokes, had felt queasy when a girl she didn't know touched her hand.

"In my opinion. That's nature, ain't it?" Shirley nodded at the turtles. "Does it have to bother you?"

Jamie found she could not get any redder than she already was. "Um, not really!"

"That's right, it don't have to fuss you. You just let the turtles do what they do, and you do what's right for you when it's time. You know what my mama used to tell me? 'Just keep your drawers up and your skirts down till you're grown.' "

Outside of the oh-so-careful health classes in school, Jamie had never met an adult who seemed willing to discuss sex of any kind, let alone turtle sex. Suddenly she felt comfortable and triumphant. She grinned at Shirley. "You're baaad!"

"I have the reputation in this neighborhood of being a wee bit eccentric," Shirley acknowledged, feeding pieces of apple and corn muffin to Otto and Mimi.

"Nooooooo. You're kidding."

"But yes. Squirrely Shirley, they call me. Nutty old spinster lady. Crazy woman with twenty-one turtles." Shirley kept grinning, but her eyes had gone sad.

"That's stupid! Like your turtles really bother people? Barking all night? Running wild and attacking little kids?"

Shirley stared, then started to laugh so hard she rocked on her haunches.

"I think your turtles are nice," Jamie grumbled, patting Bobo on his unresponsive shell, atop which his name was carefully lettered in black enamel. Shirley had thinly outlined the scales of his shell in red and blue. He looked tastefully well groomed, in Jamie's opinion, and if Shirley wanted to keep turtles and dress them up it was her business. "I wish people would just let other people alone."

"It'll never happen." Shirley was still chuckling. "Turtles don't let other turtles alone. Tell you something, turtles are a lot like people. They live long and never seem to get smarter, for one thing. You know that turtle in your lap is probably older than you are?"

"He is?"

"Probably. I've had Bobo for ten years, but God knows how old he was when I found him. He might be older than me. Box turtles live up to a hundred and thirty-eight years. Or one twenty-nine. Depending on which book you read."

"You're kidding!" Jamie sat up straight and stopped patting Bobo. Lightning might strike her for patting something so venerable. No wonder Shirley rescued turtles. Imagine letting something that could live so long get mushed on the road.

"Nope, no kidding. They're ancient. Don't let them fool you. They're not always this frisky."

About a dozen turtles had gathered sedately around Shirley, waiting to be fed. Aside from the two in the grass still clunking their shells together, Jamie saw no frisking.

"They just came out of their holes not too long ago," Shirley explained. "They hibernate over the winter, and I always pity them. Sure, it keeps them alive, but they can't like it down there in the dark. They always seem so happy and hungry when they come up to the light. Like people, again."

"Huh?"

"Oh, I don't know." Hesitating, Shirley looked up as if the sky would help her find words. "If we'd just get out of our holes, get out of ourselves . . . we all have shells and they slow us down so much."

Jamie realized she was staring, because Shirley gave her a crooked grin. "Okay, so I'm strange," Shirley said.

"No stranger than my family."

Shirley nodded in acknowledgment. "I had this funny dream about turtles once," she said. "There was a full moon, and they all gathered in the middle of the yard, only it was bigger—you know how it is in dreams; everything was a little different. The turtles were all different colors in the moonlight, lilac and black and silver and maraschino cherry. And they started to dance, but to do that they had to get out of their shells." Shirley looked at Jamie owlishly, her eyebrows steepled higher than ever. "Do you know, when they did that, they were slim like spirits and they could stand up and jump like Baryshnikov? They still had their little beady eyes and their big scaly feet, but they didn't care. They could waltz, they could fandango, they could strut their little butts. They were kind of funny looking, but whoo-ee could they dance."

In Jamie's lap, Bobo tremored like an earthquake and poked his head out into the light.

Chapter

7

Lily sat on her closet floor, facing away from the light that slanted in from the upstairs hallway. The bedroom itself was dark now, because it was after sunset, but the hallway light was on, and that well-meaning child Kate insisted that the doors be left open. Katie was a dear heart, but she just did not understand: Lily would have felt better if the door were closed, the heavy oak barriers all stoutly in place. Terrible things could happen if the barriers were opened. The closet, having three solid walls, was preferable even with its door open to the fearsome space and lucidity of the bedroom, with its glassy windows through which a person could lose herself. But it would have been better yet if the door were closed. When Kate went to bed, Lily would close the door.

When she got up to do that, she planned, she would first walk carefully to the bathroom and use the toilet. It was all right, though frightening, to leave the closet to use the toilet. Certainly Daddy would have to agree it was all right.

Daddy would approve. Daddy would approve. When Daddy had been alive, he had been like the thick oak door, strong to close out evil and its terrifying consequences. He had been the barrier between Lily and everything dangerous and forbidden that tried to make her a bad girl. But now he was gone, and the wind was always tearing at the house corners, and who knew what wrong things Lily's hands might do, what wrong words might come out of her mouth, what wrong thoughts might breach her mind?

Downstairs she heard someone at the front door—but she must not hear that. Someone she must not remember was always knocking. Someone she must not remember was always calling through the windows, calling to her, calling to her. She must not hear. Evil, evil. She must not ever hear his voice again.

Someone was—coming up the stairs!

"Mamaw?"

Lily breathed out. It was just that sweet child Kate.

"Mamaw, I'm going to turn on the light. Jamie's back."

A sudden squeezing feeling in her heart made Lily gasp. For some inexpressible reason, Lily had not truly believed that her granddaughter was ever coming back, no matter how many times Kate had said that Jamie would be back Sunday night. When the light blazed on and Lily blinked, tears ran hotly down her cheeks.

"Grandma?" She felt Jamie's strong young arms around her. "Grandma, don't cry. I just took a little bus trip, and I'm back now. Grandma, I won't go away again for a while. Why are you sitting here in the dark?"

Lily could not answer.

"Grandma, c'mon out. Come on downstairs with me." Jamie got up and tugged at Lily's arms, and Lily obeyed those commanding young hands. There was a lot of Daddy in Jamie. Lily followed Jamie down the stairs to the kitchen.

"How about something to eat? A piece of cinnamon toast? Grandma?"

"All right," Lily said. Now that she was spending most of her time in the closet, it was all right for her to eat. Daddy would approve. In the closet Lily's actions were so few that consequences seemed under control.

It was even all right for her to sit at the table and hold onto it while she let Jamie and Kate prepare the snack. At night, when darkness made a barrier against the windows, it was all right, but she could not have done it in the daytime, when daylight streaming in made her feel as weightless as dandelion fluff, without substance, so that every stray word threatened to carry her away.

Jamie would take care of her. Jamie had substance. Jamie looked tired, or maybe somber, as if she felt the weight of being a wall. Jamie knew, had to know, that she was the only thing standing between her grandma and the whole world's sorrow.

At the other end of the kitchen the girls were carrying on a whispered conversation. Lily did not try to hear what they were saying. When they came to sit with her, she continued to listen without hearing as they chatted about school. She ate her toast, and some sliced peaches they gave her, and smiled at them. She answered bravely and politely when they asked her how she was feeling. Such sweet, beautiful girls. Such a good girl, Jamie, her granddaughter. It was so much safer with a girl, a granddaughter. Jamie would not—would never . . .

Lily could not remember. Must not remember.

"Grandma," Jamie was saying to her earnestly, "I have to tell you something."

Lily sat blinking in the light. Jamie came and crouched by her chair, looking up at her, holding Lily's chilly old hands in her warm young ones, gazing into Lily's eyes.

"Grandma," Jamie said, "I've been back to Silver Valley. Do you remember Silver Valley?"

"No," Lily whispered, but it was not in answer to the question.

"Well, anyway, that's where I went," Jamie said. "Silver Valley. And guess what?" Jamie sounded gentle. Jamie was smiling but talking a little too fast. "You'll never guess. I heard about a boy with the same name as me. Well, a man now, named Jamie Bridger. Do you know him, Grandma? Is he any relation to us?"

"No," Lily whimpered, not at Jamie but at the storm. It was shaking her chest, a hurricane, roaring in her mind, a tornado, spinning the kitchen around so that the barriers were falling, falling, falling, the walls in splinters, the windows open to the sky. Punishment would come pouring in. "No!" Lily screamed, lurching up, pulling away from her granddaughter. "No! No!" She ran, staggering, nearly falling, out of the kitchen and up the dark stairs to her closet, where she cowered.

The end of the world was always knocking at the door. She must not let him in. She must not let him in. She must never come out again. She must never come out again.

"Oh, my God!" Kate whispered, gazing at the enlarged photocopies Jamie had brought back with her, gazing at the other Jamie Bridger's yearbook face. "I can't believe it! He looks so much like you!" Still staring, Kate began to smile. "He's *cute!*"

Jamie smiled a little but did not answer. It was hard to come up with something to say when she kept thinking about Grandma, Grandma, Grandma, Lily who had taken her tranquilizer pill like a good girl, Lily who was asleep upstairs on the closet floor. Jamie folded her arms on the kitchen table, laid her head down on them and sighed. "I shouldn't have said anything to her," she muttered.

Kate sighed too and put the yearbook pictures aside. "Maybe she just needs some time."

Jamie stared at the wall, trying to sort it out. If she called the doctor, would he want to put Grandma in a hospital? Would Jamie be able to keep him from doing that?

"She's not hurting anybody," Kate said, answering Jamie's thoughts. "So she's living in a bedroom closet, so what? At least she's eating now. And it's not like she's going to take a gun and kill people."

Jamie said without looking up, "Face it, Kate, she's crazy." Jamie could say this only because she knew her friend loved Grandma as much as she did.

There was a long silence before Kate admitted, "Maybe. I guess it depends on what you call crazy. But she's not dangerous."

"It's enough to make anybody crazy," Jamie said fiercely. She sat up, glaring. "Her son thrown out, and she's never supposed to mention him again—do you think that was her idea? That was Grandpa. I would like to take him and shake him and break him into little pieces."

"He's dead, doofus."

"Yeah, well, I could kill him again. He dragged her here, away from her family—the Wolgemuths said she had family that used to visit, a sister from Chicago—"

"The Wolgemuths?"

"The neighbors. Old people. They remembered me from when I was a baby." Jamie quieted down, thinking about her talk with them. "You think I'm an okay judge of people, Kate?"

"Sure. You like me." Kate grinned.

"That doesn't count," Jamie teased. "I grew up with you. I'm stuck with you." Then she got serious. "But like, Ian, I'd never met her before, but I knew she really wanted to help. And Shirley, I just knew she was okay." Jamie had already told Kate a lot about Shirley and her turtles. "Shirley is great. But the Wolgemuths—they seemed nice, but I got the feeling they didn't want to talk to me."

"Why not?"

Jamie gave her friend an exasperated look. "Like I know? Maybe they just don't like teenagers." She hesitated. "But I got the feeling they knew something they didn't want to tell me."

"Like what?"

"Kate, give me a break! If I knew what, I—I might see a way out of this mess."

The two of them sat silently. The dowdy house seemed very quiet, the way Grandma was quiet and dowdy most of the time. In the next room the grandfather clock was ticking.

"I've got to do something," Jamie whispered. "If people find out how bad Grandma is, they'll send her to a mental hospital and me to a home or something. I've got to find some answers."

"You did do something," Kate told her softly. "You found out a lot."

"Yeah, most of it bad. I found out my grandfather was a total son of a bitch. I found out I might have a father, but he ran away and only came back and tried to find me once."

Kate said sternly, "Jamie, lighten up. He was a kid."

"So am I, a kid." Jamie found herself blinking back tears. "Why am I stuck with all this? I need to find Jamie Bridger, but I can't leave Grandma alone when she's like this. What am I going to do?"

Kate surprised her by smiling a big, warm, slow smile. "You'll think of something," she said, getting up and hugging Jamie good-night before she went home. "I know you."

Starting the next morning, Jamie did what she could think of.

She biked to the Dexter Public Library, asked to see a Chicago telephone directory, and found the number for the courthouse. As Shirley had suggested, she phoned, asking for the information in her birth-certificate file. She was told to submit her request to the prothonotary in writing. She did so, but knew she could not expect a response for days, maybe weeks. By then Grandma would be in a mental hospital. She had to find Jamie Bridger.

While she had the Chicago directory, she looked up everybody named Bridger or Lutz. Over the next two days she phoned them all. None of them knew a Cletus Bridger or a Lily Lutz. Or an Amaryllis Lutz, which was what the Wolgemuths thought Grandma's sister's name might have been. The sister was married, though, and even if she was still in Chicago, her last name wasn't Lutz anymore.

One of the people she talked with suggested she might want to try the Salvation Army. She called them, and they said yes, they searched for missing family members, and they sent her forms to fill out. She sent back two—one for Amaryllis Lutz and one for Jamie Bridger.

She phoned Ian, and got Ian's father's number, and phoned him in Florida, and talked with him for a while. When she hung up, she had that odd feeling again: There was something he did not want to tell her.

She went through Grandpa's desk again, finding nothing that helped. She searched his bedroom, Grandma's bedroom, the kitchen and basement and attic, opening drawers and boxes, looking for something, a stray envelope maybe, or old letters, or an old address book, any piece of paper that might give her a name, a clue, an address. There was nothing.

She phoned the Dexter police. They told her they couldn't help her. She slammed down the phone, then cooled off and tried the state police. They told her the same thing.

She phoned the tooth factory and asked them to look in her Grandpa's records and tell her where he used to work. Then she phoned Product Technical Services outside of Silver Valley and asked for anybody who could tell her anything about former employee Cletus Bridger or his family. Nobody remembered him.

She knew Grandpa's birthplace, from the obituary. She phoned 555-1212 and asked for any Bridgers or Lutzes listed there. None were.

She studied the amount in Grandma's bank account, then called a private detective. "How old are you?" he asked. She told him. "You're wasting my time," he said, and he hung up on her.

She phoned Shirley. "This is Jamie."

Shirley seemed not the least bit surprised. "Jamie, good to hear from you. How's it going, kiddo?"

"Awful." Jamie poured it all out. "I'm trying everything to find my father, and nothing works. I'm getting behind in all my subjects, and the school is talking about sending a truant officer. Grandma just sits in the closet, and I try to talk with her, but she just smiles and says yes and no and oh dear. I'm doing all the laundry and shopping and cooking—"

"Whoa," Shirley said. "Back up, and explain to me about Grandma in the closet."

Jamie did. "I have to find the other Jamie Bridger." Most of her waking thoughts and a lot of her dreams were focused on finding Jamie Bridger. She wanted a father. She wanted a hero, a rescuing savior. If losing him had

83

made Grandma crazy, wouldn't getting him back make her well again?

"Yes, I'm sure you do," Shirley said slowly, "but don't expect him to ride in on a white horse and fix everything, Jamie."

"I've got to find him!"

"Tell me what you've tried so far."

Jamie did.

"Damn good job," Shirley said. "One thing, though. If he's alive and in this country, you might be able to trace him through his credit record."

"Huh?"

"Most people use credit cards."

"They do?" Grandpa never did.

"Yes, they do. Believe me. And there are credit bureaus—"

"And they wouldn't want a kid wasting their time," Jamie interrupted bitterly. She had been having trouble sleeping, and went around all day every day with her chest aching. She needed to find Jamie Bridger; her small supply of patience was entirely used up on Grandma, and she had none left for the stupidity of other adults. Luckily, Shirley seemed to understand a lot of this.

"You'll have to find someone to get his credit record for you," she said without a sign that she had noticed Jamie's rude tone. "Do you know anybody who works in the loan office of a bank?"

Jamie did not. But she called Ian, and Ian did.

It took some doing. Just the name, Jamie Lee Bridger, was not enough. Jamie had to call Silver Valley High School and persuade a secretary to search the old school

84

records for the other Jamie's birthdate and Social Security number.

Then she had to go around whispering, "Please" to the sky for what seemed like forever.

Only a few hours, actually. Ian called her back the same day. "Jackpot," Ian sang. "Aren't fax machines wonderful?"

"You found him?!"

"Just an address. Looks like Jamie's in the Big Apple. New York City." Ian read the address to her. Jamie made her spell everything and read everything twice. Then she thanked Ian, hung up the phone and stood taking deep breaths to try to calm down. She was trembling.

This was it. Closer than she had ever been.

She tiptoed upstairs and checked on her grandmother. Lily sat leaning against one wall of her closet, staring at the other wall and tunelessly humming. She would stay that way for hours. Jamie tiptoed back to the phone again. Picked it up with a hand that shook.

"Hello, information?"

A minute later she was shaking even harder, this time with frustration and rage. There was no listing for any Jamie Bridger in New York City or vicinity.

"I can't believe it!"

It was time for Kate to come home from school. Jamie stomped out to meet her, not caring that she let the door bang.

"I can't *believe* after all this he has an unlisted number!"

"What? Who?" Kate stood wide-eyed on the sidewalk.

"Jamie Pain-in-the-Butt Bridger! He's in New York

City somewhere. Kate, can you stay with Grandma this weekend?" Jamie's tone veered from furious to pleading. "She can't get much worse than she already is. I have to go find him."

"Jamie, are you *crazy*? In New York City?"

"Kate, *please*! I have to! Look, all I have to do is take a taxi from the bus station and go to the address. If I don't find him, I'll just turn around and take a bus home. I won't stay overnight. I won't get into any trouble. Kate?"

Kate stood looking at her with worried eyes.

"Please, Kate?"

"As if I could make you not do it," Kate grumped. She blew out a long breath. "All right. But you be real careful, Jamie, you hear?"

Chapter

The bus trip to New York was a long one, six hours, and Jamie sat hunched forward the whole time, clutching between her knees the tote bag Kate had insisted on in case she got stranded, chewing her nails and trying not to think. If she let herself think, she would be sick right in her lap; she knew it. *Don't think.*

Could she find him? Would he answer her knock at the door? What would she say if he did? "Listen, I'm Jamie Bridger too, and I think you're my—"

Don't think.

In the city the crowds and traffic and noise made the knot in Jamie's chest pull yet tighter. There were dirty white flutters of trash everywhere—that bothered her. At home Mrs. Leweski would have picked it all up, no matter how long it took. Under the trash everything looked gray to Jamie, and there was a gray buzzing feeling in her head from exhaust fumes. Even the birds were gray. Sparrows. Pigeons.

I don't belong here.

And people seemed to know she didn't belong. She must have been doing something wrong, or else being an out-of-town kid with a tote bag was wrong, because the taxis would not stop for her. Once one finally pulled over, the driver barely spoke English. She had to tell him the address twice, then sit with her fists clenched and hope he knew where he was going.

The traffic moved unlike any traffic Jamie had previously experienced, not in lanes but in blobs and stops and stampedes. Inches from another taxi her driver gestured and cursed—in a foreign language, but Jamie could tell it was cursing. The meter muttered and mumbled to itself the whole time whether her taxi was moving or not, doing its sums.

Abruptly the driver pulled over at a corner. "Here go," he said.

He meant—was this it? Rattled, Jamie got out, pulled her money out of her jeans pocket and paid him the unbelievable amount that was winking on the meter. The taxi driver sat looking at her a minute, but she was not paying attention; she was staring around at a bewilderment of buildings. She was just about to try to ask the taxi driver which one it was when he made an angry noise in his throat, then roared away.

The names on the street sign seemed unrelated to the address she wanted. Jamie had no idea which direction to walk but started walking anyway, trying to look more like a New Yorker and less like a hick from the sticks. This seemed like a quieter section than the crowded area around the Port Authority. There weren't many people on the sidewalks here, and the ones Jamie saw were hurrying and scowling. There were no shops, no shopkeepers Jamie could ask for directions, just blocky buildings that must be office buildings and—apartments, one of them the other Jamie Bridger's apartment building. So close. Jamie was too nervous to think straight. The few building numbers she saw seemed to be about right, but where was the street?

Jamie came to another street sign. The street numbers seemed to be getting farther away from the one she wanted. Feeling very lost, she turned around and started back the way she had come, hurrying now, scowling with worry. This city was too big, too gray, and where were all the people when she needed them?

But half a block past the corner where her taxi had originally left her, she began with a surge of relief to understand. There was construction, the road torn up, her taxi would not have been able to get through. The number street she needed would be the next one. And the building, judging by the building numbers she had seen on the other streets, would be—there. Looking up ahead and off to her right, Jamie could see a brick apartment building that might be it.

Across a vacant lot from her.

A vacant lot surrounded by a high plywood fence. But there were boards torn off to make an entry, and a path worn into the weeds and rubble on the other side. People went through here.

Instinctively Jamie ducked in to go that way, not so much because it was a shortcut as because it was a space in the city, and her chest needed space, air, green. There were plantain and dandelions making soft hills of the rubble where something had been torn down. There were sumac bushes. Dime-sized yellow clover heads blooming around all sorts of trash. Chicory growing through somebody's dead shirt matted onto the ground.

Her mind on her destination, Jamie did not so much observe any of this as sense it—a hint of country, even here. Wildflowers insistent, like hope. Jamie's shoulders unhunched for the first time in hours, opening like wings so that she breathed more freely. Eagerly she strode toward where she hoped to find the other Jamie Bridger.

Broken bricks underfoot, amid daisies. A corner of what used to be a brick gas station or something still standing. The path went around it. Jamie followed the path—

"Hand it over," a hard voice said. A narrow-faced man in dirty jeans stood glowering at her, blocking her way.

Kate stood looking out Mamaw's living-room window, watching the real estate agent put up a FOR SALE sign on the Garibay front lawn, wishing she could go rip it out and throw it in the garbage and that would make a difference. This was one time when talking with her parents for hours hadn't helped; they felt they had to move away, but Kate just didn't want to. Mostly because of Jamie. Even if Jamie hadn't been in sixteen kinds of difficulties, Kate would have felt that way.

She sighed, not looking forward to the moment when Jamie saw that stupid sign. Kate had put off telling Jamie and put off telling Jamie, but now she would not be able to put off telling her any longer. It was all settled. Her mother and father had found a place in the rich eastern Pennsylvania farm country not far from the state capital. Moving date was coming up in less than a month.

Jamie ought to be in New York by now. Kate sighed again, this time with worry. Being afraid of the big city was so small-town, so uncool, but still—Kate hoped Jamie was okay.

The phone rang.

Kate jumped, then ran to answer it, her heart thumping. Jamie had promised she would call when she had news.

"Hello?"

"Hello, Jamie, this is Ian," said a bright and breezy voice.

"Oh, hi, Ian. This isn't Jamie, this is Kate." As if Ian knew who Kate was. "I'm taking care of things here while she's away," she added by way of explanation, feeling herself cloud up with worrying about Jamie again. "Jamie went to New York to try to find her father."

"She did?" Ian sounded surprised, but not as anxious as Kate. "I thought she'd write him first. Well, I've got a letter from him."

"You *do*?"

"Uh-huh. He wrote the high school a couple weeks back asking them to get him in touch with his class, and they just now forwarded his letter to me. Those birdbrains at the school office had his address and phone number the whole time." Ian sounded more bemused than annoyed. "They could have given it to Jamie when she called."

Kate was neither bemused nor annoyed—she was furious for Jamie's sake. Jamie could have had the information she needed a couple of weeks ago. Jamie was blundering around in New York when she could have just phoned—but Kate forced herself to be calm. "Why don't you give me the phone number, and I'll see that she gets it."

"Okay, certainly." Ian read it off while Kate wrote it down. "You'll be sure to tell her I called?"

"Sure." As soon as she could get rid of Ian, Kate picked up the phone again and dialed the number Ian had given her, with no idea what she was going to say. She couldn't tell this man things Jamie should tell him herself, but she felt like she had to do something. Maybe Jamie would be there already, and Kate would be able to stop worrying. Or maybe she would just tell the other Jamie Bridger that Jamie was on the way to see him about something important, and he should stay close to the doorbell. That was it. She would make sure he stayed home and waited for Jamie.

Three rings, four, five. Please, somebody answer. Eight rings, nine, ten. Somebody pick up the phone? *Please?*

But nobody did. There was nobody home. Oh damn, double damn, triple damn, nobody was going to be there when Jamie got there.

"Hand it over!" the narrow-faced man said again, louder and harder, keeping one hand in the pocket of his dirty jeans as if he had something there—a knife, a gun?

Used to walking by herself in the woods, Jamie had seldom in her life thought about predators. There just weren't that many in Dexter, but now—stunned by surprise, taken off guard, she had not reacted, and the man in dirty jeans was getting upset. Hand it over? One moment she had been finding a father and the next minute this angry stranger was in her face, frightening her, she couldn't think, nothing made sense, and the only thing in her hand was her tote bag—he wanted it for some reason? She held it out to him.

He snatched it with his left hand, keeping his right hand in his pocket. He tossed it up, caught it by the corner and dumped it. A plastic bag of animal crackers, a ham sandwich wrapped in wax paper, photocopies of yearbook pictures of Jamie Bridger, spare T-shirt and undies, all tumbled down and lay amid bricks and daisies. The man in dirty jeans kicked aside the clothing, the sandwich, the papers.

"Bitch! Where's your money?" His right hand jumped out of his pocket, empty but curled into a fist. He punched her in the face.

Jamie screamed. She had never in her life been a screamer, but she had never in her life been so shocked and hurt and furious either. Even more furious than scared. Screaming with fury, she tried to hit him back. But he was stronger than she was. He punched her again, in the eye.

"Hand it over! Now!"

She could see nothing but black-and-red special effects, but she could hear him yelling in her ear, and she could hear herself screeching like a wildcat, and no way was she handing anything over. Who the hell did he think he was? Just because he was bigger than she was, he thought he could hit her, take the money she needed to get home? Jamie was so mad she didn't think what might happen, just flailed out blindly at him. And she kicked, feeling the toe of her sneaker connect where she hoped it hurt.

Maybe it did, because he yelled, "You crazy slut! I'll kill you!" He swung again.

"Let her alone!" somebody shouted. Blurrily Jamie saw another man running across the vacant lot toward her. Then Dirty Jeans walloped her a nasty one. She fell to the brick-strewn ground.

But Jamie did not mind, because it was the last time he hit her. And looking up past a tuft of daisies she had quite a dramatic view as Jamie Bridger stepped over her and punched the mugger, nice and hard, in the jaw.

"Ow," Bridger complained, mocking and scorching mad. "You hurt my hand." He punched again, a solid uppercut. He looked older than his yearbook pictures, of course, and a lot tougher, bending the bad guy double with a gut punch. But Jamie knew him. She would have known him anywhere.

"Get out," he said to Dirty Jeans, giving him a shove. The mugger took the hint and scuttled away toward the hole in the fence. Somebody else, a curly-haired bear of a blond man, was bending over Jamie, but she hardly looked at him. Her whole attention was fixed on Bridger, Jamie Bridger, standing there tall and spraddle-legged, his shoulders lifting as he took in a long breath, settling as he blew it out to blow away his anger. His hands relaxed, no longer curled into fists. He turned around.

Jamie struggled to sit up, making it only halfway.

"Wait," Bridger told her. "Don't move." He started toward her.

"Jamie," she said to him.

For a moment everything just stopped. He froze, staring at her. The blond man, picking up Jamie's things from the ground, froze with a sheet of paper in his hand.

Arms braced to steady herself, Jamie said in a voice that was not quite working smoothly. "You're Jamie Bridger. My name's Jamie Bridger too."

"Bridge," said the blond man, "look." He was holding up one of Jamie's yearbook photocopies. "She knows you. She was probably coming to see you."

Bridger glanced wide-eyed from Jamie to his own teenage photocopied face to Jamie again, stunned, bewildered—his mouth opened without speaking. Jamie wanted to get up and go to him and tell him it was all right. She tried to heave herself off the ground. But Bridger exclaimed, "Whoa!" and strode over to kneel beside her. "Lie still," he said. "First things first."

She liked his voice, quiet and gruff, but she had her own ideas of first things. Her thoughts were moving like Shirley's turtles, slow but intent on what they wanted. She said to Bridger, "Are you my father?"

"Shhh. Don't try to talk." With one hand he reached out and lightly touched her head, tilting it a little, looking her over for injuries. "Your nose is bleeding." He turned to his friend. "David, you got any Kleenex?"

"Like I carry Kleenex?"

Bridger rolled his eyes and reached for something cottony and pink lying on the ground, but when he tried to dab at Jamie with it, she pulled back.

"That's my spare underpants."

"Good lord, I'll buy you more underpants, okay? We better get you inside. Can you walk?"

Jamie held the makeshift hankie to her nose as Bridger lifted her under one arm, David under the other. On her feet she swayed like the daisies. Still hanging onto her, Bridger scooped up her tote bag and steered her forward. He and his friend supported her between them as she walked none too steadily across the vacant lot, around a corner, through a doorway, into a vestibule. Time had blurred. Standing in the elevator required concentration. She heard low-voiced conversation without really listening: Damn lucky the guy didn't have a gun. Should we call the cops? What good would it do? Suppose she's a runaway? Let me talk with her first. Some time later she blinked with surprise and discovered that she was no longer standing in the elevator, but lying on a sofa in Bridger's apartment. It was a classy-looking place, decorated Art Deco style, with lots of pink and gray and shiny surfaces. But Jamie did not remember walking in.

Bridger came out of what might have been the kitchen and hurried across the room to her, carrying wads of cotton and a bag of crushed ice. He sat on the edge of the sofa beside her, packed her nose with the cotton, felt at it to make sure it was not broken, then carefully positioned the ice on it. "You took a couple of really nasty shots," he said.

"I'm okay."

"Don't try to move. Is your vision blurry?"

"No."

"Follow my finger with your eyes." He moved it from

side to side, then down and up. Jamie had no trouble tracking it. "Do you remember what happened?" Bridger asked her.

"Sure. Mugger slugged me."

Bridger smiled. It was a beautiful smile, wide as sunrise and warm as sunshine. "You're okay."

David came and stood beside Bridger, handing him three different kinds of antiseptic. Bridger leaned over Jamie and began cautiously to dab at the damage. He was very gentle for a guy who could punch so hard. "Just relax and close your eyes," he said in that gruff voice of his, and it sounded like a wonderful idea. Jamie closed her eyes, lay still and breathed deeply through her mouth, letting him take care of her. Being taken care of felt good. After everything that had been happening, it felt like the first time anybody had taken care of her in the history of the world.

"Jamie?" she whispered after a while.

"Nobody calls me that anymore," he said quietly, removing the cotton from her nose. "There, you seem to be done bleeding. Call me Bridger. Or Bridge."

She opened her eyes to look at him. "Bridge—my name is Jamie Bridger too."

"You said that before. It's freaking the hell out of me."

"You look just like me."

"I noticed. That's freaking me silly too."

Jamie said, "Somebody named me after you, and I don't think it was Grandma and Grandpa."

He had finished with her face and was watching her intently. "Grandma and Grandpa who?"

97

"Bridger. Cletus Uru Bridger. Resurrection Lily Bridger."

"My parents," he murmured.

"I know. They raised me. Are you my father?"

He took her hand and said very softly, "Jamie, can we table that for just a little while? Till you're feeling better?"

"I'm fine." She lifted the ice off her nose and sat up to face him, wobbling only a little. "Please. I've got to know."

"I wish I was. You are one gutsy kid." But he sat there holding her hand and wearily shaking his head.

"You—you're not?"

"No."

But—this couldn't be happening. "You have to be," Jamie insisted. Nothing made any sense otherwise. "Could—is it even a little bit possible? Maybe you didn't know—"

"Jamie," he interrupted gently, "there is no possible way I can be your father."

"But—"

"Look at me. Read my lips." The warmth of his hand and the sadness of his smile took the sting out of this. "Jamie, I—assuming you know where babies come from —it can't be me. I have never had sex with a woman. No woman. Ever."

It was such a bizarre, extreme day that this did not embarrass her. But it did surprise her, because he was very good-looking. She sat there staring at him with her mouth open. "You—you're a virgin?"

Looking back at her, his eyes winced. His face went pink. He looked down at the carpet.

Then his friend, David, the big blond man, walked over and put a hand protectively on his shoulder, looking levelly at Jamie.

"Oh," she whispered, getting it. "Oh."

Bridger nodded.

"They—he—threw you out because—"

He looked up at her again. "Because I'm gay. Yes."

It made sense; it was just what Grandpa would do— but nothing made sense. "Great," Jamie whispered, and then she heard herself shouting it. "Oh, just great!" She was on her feet, shouting. "Just wonderful! My grandpa eats stewed chicken and dies and my grandma is sitting on her big butt in a closet and I'm failing school, I never have time to do art anymore, the checkbook is totally screwed up and I come all the way to New York and forget to tip the cabdriver and now you're gay! Where's my father, where's my mother? Who are they?" Her head ached, her face hurt, her throat hurt from shouting, everything hurt. She started to sob. "I want—somebody."

"Jamie. Shhhh." Bridge stood up and put his arms around her, and she was hanging onto him and sobbing on his shoulder, and he was patting her back, soothing her shoulders. "Easy, Jamie. Easy." He felt big, strong, solid, warm, his hands warm on her back, his face warm against her head. "We'll work on it," he told her. "We'll figure it out, I promise you. We'll find out who you are."

Chapter

9

"Could you have a brother or sister you don't know about?" Jamie asked Bridger. "Could that be where I came from?"

"Not likely." But Bridge spread his hands. "A few hours ago I would have said no way, not in a thousand years, but now I'm not sure of anything." Jamie had been telling him her story, and he looked stunned, dazed by the implications. "They withheld important information from you. Maybe they withheld important information from me."

From where she sat at Bridge and David's dining table, Jamie could see her reflection in their mirrored wall, and the sight of herself made her wince. Swollen mouth, bruised cheek, black eye—she looked awful. Yet she felt fine in a what-a-day sort of way. Her belly was full of David's good veal tetrazzini. She had phoned Kate to tell her she was okay. She was going to bunk on the sofa for the night, and Bridge was going back to Dexter with her in the morning. She had gotten silly trying to explain to Kate that Bridge was not her father after all, but he was still Grandma's son, and he wanted to see her. Which he did, very much. He did not seem to believe how nuts Grandma was. *My whole life is nuts,* Jamie thought. *Surreal.* So surreal, she no longer felt very teary. Mostly she felt interested in how strange things were.

"Maybe I'm really some sort of cousin or something."

David came in from rinsing plates and said, "This is starting to sound like a logic problem, and I have often wondered whether logic can be applied to Bridger."

"David is a data analyst on Wall Street." Bridge smiled and reached for pen and paper. "Let's see if he can analyze this situation." He wrote down:

POSSIBILITIES LIST
Jamie is child of unknown brother or sister.
Jamie is some sort of cousin or something.

"Good grief," Jamie whispered, watching. "Your handwriting is just like mine."

"So we're time-warp twins, so what else is new?"

Jamie said, "Maybe a mad scientist stole body cells from you and kept them for fourteen years and did a sex change on them and made them into me."

"I am not going to write that down," Bridger complained.

"Or maybe we're both aliens."

Bridger rolled his eyes, but David laughed so heartily he stamped his feet. "I like it! It fits."

101

"This is not one of your sci-fi novels," Bridger grumbled. "Don't get him started, Jamie."

Jamie said, "Okay, how's this one. You had sex with a woman and you don't remember. Like, you got drunk."

"I don't drink."

"Okay, you've got amnesia."

Bridger sighed and pushed the list away. "This isn't working."

"Maybe I'm adopted," Jamie said. "Maybe I'm no relation to you at all." Damn, her voice was going ragged. "Maybe I'm never going to have a family."

"Now you listen." Bridge leaned forward and took her by the shoulders, looking straight into her eyes. "No matter what we find out, you're precious to me, understand? Good grief, we both have the same name, we look alike, we were raised by the same neurotic people. That's more connected than most families ever get."

Jamie gazed back at him and felt herself smiling but could not speak.

"I am so pissed that nobody told me about you when I went back." Bridger let go of her to clench his fists. "Those damn tight-ass neighbors, I could fry them in oil. Them and that snotty lawyer. They'd guessed about me, or heard about me, I could see it in their eyes, and they wouldn't tell me anything. Polite pricks."

"That was the same feeling I got," Jamie said, trying to straighten out her loopy smile. At least her voice was behaving now. "They weren't telling me things."

"Yeah, well, screw them all. We're going to find out the truth. And I think what we're going to find out is that we're related somehow, Jamie." Bridge leaned back, and his smile was just as wide and loopy as hers. "I'd like that. I want family too."

"If we can find Grandma's sister Amaryllis," Jamie said. "I bet she can tell us something."

"Aunt Mary!" Bridge stopped smiling and sat up straight. "That's right, her real name was Amaryllis. Amaryllis Duncan. I would have tried to get in touch with her years ago, but I couldn't remember where she was from."

"Someplace around Chicago, the Wolgemuths said. But they didn't tell me her last name."

"Duncan, I'm sure it was Duncan. Aunt Mary and Uncle Don Duncan." Bridge got up and paced around the room, he was so excited, but he did not go near the phone. "We'll track her down, Jamie, but—but not right now. Can you wait one more day?" He turned to her, appealing. "I want to see Ma first."

"Sure."

"I know she's in bad shape, but I'm a never-say-die dreamer, okay? Deep down she knows where she got you from, and I'm still hoping she'll tell us herself."

David stood watching from across the room as Bridger gave Jamie another ibuprofen and asked her if she had brushed her teeth and brought blankets to the sofa for her. The tough guy actually tucked her in. Sure, Bridge was a nurse, and a good one, but from what David could see, the way Bridge felt about Jamie was even more than the way a good nurse cared about somebody who had been hurt.

"G'night," Bridge told Jamie softly. "Holler if you need anything, all right?"

She did not answer. Already asleep, or nearly asleep. Worn out. What a day for her.

What a day.

Bridge padded across the carpet to David and touched him on the shoulder. The two of them walked softly to their room.

"You okay, buddy?" Bridge asked, keeping his voice down.

David told an untruth. "I'm fine."

"Well, I'm not. I'm flabbergasted." Bridger sat on the edge of the bed, his eyes round. "I get up this morning, just another day in the life, Saturday off, I have lunch, do a little shopping, I'm walking home and there's a commotion and zap, kazowie, things are never going to be the same. Where the hell did she come from? Who is she? Did you ever hear of anything so weird?"

David had an idea he knew who Jamie was, but he just shook his head, sitting on the thick charcoal-gray carpet to listen to Bridge babbling. The only other time he had ever heard Bridge talk this much was one night when there had been a particularly ugly death in the emergency room where Bridge worked. There was nothing ugly about Jamie, but still—Bridge was in shock.

"I gotta pack." Bridge stood up and went to his dresser, rooting through its drawers in a useless way. "Better take a suitcase, I guess. Gotta call my supervisor in the morning."

"Here." David got up and gently pushed Bridge back

to his seat on the bed. "I'll do it." He started to organize a toiletries bag for Bridge.

"I might have to stay a few days," Bridger said.

David nodded, keeping his eyes on what he was doing. He had known Bridger for only a few months, but badly wanted to know him forever. He was frightened. He wanted to say, Please don't go. He wanted to say, Please come back soon. Please come back. Don't let them take you away from me.

He said nothing, because he loved Bridger, and loving Bridger meant letting Bridger do what he had to do. Time would tell whether Bridger loved him.

"It's so strange," Bridge was saying. "Every time I look at her, it's like déjà vu, you know? Like looking back on my own childhood. I mean, I know Jamie is Jamie, she's herself, not me, and I know I'm going to learn to appreciate her that way, but for right now—comforting her is like comforting myself, consoling her is like consoling myself. I feel about fourteen years old, but it's like—I'm finally going to be able to heal the inner child in me, you know?" A moment's silence, then Bridger made a face. "God, I sound like a TV psychologist."

"Not really," David said. "You sound more like a person telling the goddamn truth."

The six-hour bus ride back to Dexter went fast for Jamie, because she and Bridge talked almost the whole way. They talked about Grandma's strawberry pies. They talked about Grandpa's waffle-potato-noodle-stuffing-stewed chicken dinners. They talked about the house in Silver

Valley, and the front room where Jamie had slept, which had been Bridger's room also. They talked about Bridger locked out and crying in a toolshed. They talked about New York City. They talked about Jamie's art. They talked about TV shows they liked, movies, books they had both read. They told each other stupid jokes, and laughed so loud that people looked at them. They found that in many deep ways, and small ones too, they understood each other. By the time they got to the outskirts of Dexter, Jamie felt as if she had always known Bridger.

"Almost there," she told him. Then she noticed his face had lost its color. "You okay?" she asked him, thinking maybe he was going to be sick. Bus fumes always made her sick, except today.

"Scared," Bridger said.

"Hey," she told him tough-kid-style, "the old man is dead. And even if he wasn't, you're a fighter now. You could whip his butt."

"I know." He managed a tense smile. "That's why I learned to box, so nobody could ever throw me out in the cold again. But funny thing." He lost his smile. "It doesn't help."

"What doesn't help?"

"Being able to wallop people. It just doesn't cut it. It—it's not what I really want."

Jamie knew what he wanted, and knew he was not likely to get it, and could not think what to say.

"I'm scared of—of seeing Ma."

There really was nothing to say.

"Jamie." He turned to her, his face tight. "What do

you think, really, about me—my being gay? Truth. Does it bother you?"

Maybe it would later, when she had time to think; maybe it would bother her some. But at that moment it honest to God did not. Jamie said, "Bridge, my life is so screwy right now that having a gay virgin for a father seems normal."

His jaw dropped, and then he leaned back in his seat and banged his head against the window glass and laughed. He laughed all the way to the bus depot.

It was a long walk from there to the house, and the walking seemed to relax him. He looked around Dexter with interest. "*Hideous* town," he said with a sort of awe. By the time he and Jamie got to the mailbox with CLETUS U. BRIDGER stenciled on it, Bridge looked ready.

Jamie, however, had seen the sign that had appeared in Kate's front yard, and felt far from ready to deal with anything.

Kate met the two of them at the front door and hugged Jamie hard. "I kept putting off telling you," she said.

"Later," Jamie told her.

"What happened to your face? Somebody hit you. You didn't tell me somebody hit you!"

There was a lot Jamie had not yet told her. "Later. Is Grandma okay?"

"About the same."

"Is it okay for Bridge to come in? She's not going to come downstairs and run into him, is she?"

"Not likely. She hasn't come downstairs all weekend."

Bridger was already in, setting his suitcase by the door, looking around with his face very still, as if he were listening to voices nobody else could hear. When Kate said hi to him he smiled at her, but the smile left quickly. His eyes left her to scan the room.

"I remember things," he murmured. "The green lamp. That corner shelf." He took a few steps toward it. "That stupid china horse. I used to love that china horse." It was a homely blue-brown thing with one hind leg broken and glued back together. "I broke it, playing with it when I wasn't supposed to. Mama fixed it quick and didn't tell Pa."

"She never told me how it got broken," Jamie said. Did Grandma remember? Why had she kept the horse? Did she ever look at it and secretly think of her lost boy?

Silence. *What now?* Jamie was wondering, but she set her stuff down and waited.

"God, it feels like the old man's still in here." Bridge hunched his shoulders, shuddering.

"He's not," Jamie said rather sharply. Even in midafternoon there was never enough sunshine in Dexter to drive the shadows out of the corners. She did not like this shadowy house or this room with the recliner where Grandpa had died, and she did not like what Bridge had said.

He did not look at her, but at the china horse. "Ma's in the closet upstairs," he said.

Both Kate and Jamie nodded, though it was not really a question.

Bridge stood with an intent look on his face. "She's

frightened," he said mostly to himself, and he headed for the stairs.

He padded up quietly on his sneakered feet. Kate and Jamie looked at each other, then followed.

It was mostly dark up there. Shades were drawn— Grandma wanted it that way. She seemed to be afraid of the window glass, the brightness, and Bridge seemed to know it. He did not turn on a light.

"Ma?"

She did not answer, but there was a scraping sound from the far side of the dim bedroom. Jamie could vaguely see Grandma's feet in their old-lady oxfords as she pulled them farther into the closet. She could see Grandma's thick legs in their support hose. The rest of Grandma was a squat shape hiding behind housedress skirts, huddled in a corner.

Bridger got down on the floor to make himself less tall. "Ma," he said. His voice sounded unsteady, and he let it tremble; he let it go up high and quavery. "Ma, it's dark in here. I'm scared." He started to cross the room toward her on his knees.

"Ma. Mama. Don't let him get me."

There was a sound like a sob from the closet, and Grandma's voice whispered hoarsely across the shadows, "Jamie?"

Outside the door, the girl Jamie Bridger could barely stand still and watch. She grabbed for Kate's hand and held on.

"It's me, Ma." Bridge had tears in his voice.

"Jamie!" Grandma cried out the name. "Oh, Jamie, are you all right? You mustn't come in here."

Bridge stopped where he was, in the middle of the bedroom. "It's cold, Ma, and it's dark, and I'm scared." He meant it. Even though it was a June afternoon, to Bridger it was that terrible night in January. He was remembering, and letting himself feel the pain. His voice quivered with pain. "Ma, I need you." He sank down on the braided rug. "Ma. Mama. Please, you've got to come out and help me."

Bridge hugged himself, sitting on the rug, swaying, bent over. Was he crying? In the dim light it was hard to tell, but Jamie thought so. She bit her lip and took a step toward him, but Kate held her back. "Wait," Kate whispered.

Jamie waited. It might have been a minute, a long minute, silent except for the sound of someone sobbing— Grandma? To Jamie the time seemed like an hour.

"Mama," Bridger begged.

"Jamie, no." She was crying hard. "Daddy— wouldn't—"

"*Mama!*"

And his mother came to him.

The housedresses swayed as if a winter wind had blown through, and their metal hangers rattled as Resurrection Lily Lutz Bridger surged up from their folds and lunged toward her son. With shaky old hands she touched his head. She toppled to her arthritic knees beside him and pulled him into her arms. Bridge clung to her, hiding his face against her shoulder.

"It's okay, honey," Grandma said to him, weeping. "It's okay, sweetie. He's gone, he's not coming back. It was a terrible time, I know it was a terrible time, but it's over. He'll never be mean to you again."

Bridge lifted his head to look at her, and kissed her on her softly wrinkled cheeks, and tears were streaking his face but he was smiling with joy, alight like a bride with joy. It was a home-again moment for him.

For Grandma too. She had her son back, and she had come out of hiding for him.

Jamie whispered, "It's going to be okay! She's going to be okay!" She grabbed Kate and hugged her. Then she could not stand still any longer. She wanted to sing, jump, dance, shout. She wanted to open all the window blinds and let the daylight in, and throw open the windows themselves and let in the fresh summer air. But most of all she wanted to hug Grandma and Bridger, so she did that first.

She ran to them and flung one arm around Grandma and one around Bridge, hugging them hard, both at once. Bridge hugged her back—she could feel his chest heaving with emotion. He hugged her like crazy and kissed her on the side of her head.

But Grandma did not hug back. Grandma just looked at her.

Lily stopped crying, and looked at Jamie serenely. Polite, yet cautious around this somewhat disreputable person with the clothing that had been slept in and the bruised face, she pulled away. With dignity she got to her feet. Bridge and Jamie stood up with her, but Lily moved farther from Jamie, closer to her tall, strong son. She turned to him with utter trust that he would protect her.

Gesturing toward the girl who had hugged her, she asked him, "Who is this?"

His face grew still. He said quietly, "I was hoping you would tell me."

"No." The glance Lily gave Jamie was not unfriendly, but she shook her head. "No, I don't believe I know her," Grandma said. "I don't believe we've met."

Chapter

10

"Jamie, I am truly sorry," Bridge said to her. "I never expected this to happen."

Sitting at Kate's kitchen table, Jamie put her head down on her arms to shut him out. Across the way she could see Grandma in the sunset-lighted sink window, humming and washing dishes after having cooked a wonderful kielbasa-and-noodles supper including peach crisp for dessert. Grandma was suddenly acting like Grandma again—but only to Bridge. She was treating Jamie as Bridger's guest and would not let her help with the cleanup. Jamie had escaped to Kate's, but Bridge had followed her there.

"All I was thinking about was getting her to connect with me again," Bridger said. "I never dreamed she would disconnect from you."

Hearing him, not looking at him, she felt his hand touch her elbow. She jerked her arm away.

"Jamie, c'mon," said another voice, Kate's voice. "I

know you're bummed," Kate said gently, "but you're not being fair. It's not Bridger's fault. Who could have known what would happen?"

Who could have known Jamie would find herself with her whole life flipped upside down, kicking like a turtle on its back?

"I should have." The table shifted as Bridge sat down. "I should have seen it coming."

Jamie lifted her head and looked hard at him. He looked back, his blue eyes somber.

"I'm a nurse," he said. "I'm supposed to know something about people."

"What's the matter with her, then?" Jamie asked harshly.

"She's . . . I don't want to put a label on it, but for some reason something in her life hurts too much. There's something she can't face at all. So she's told herself more and more lies to avoid it, and now she doesn't know what's real anymore."

"I told you that before!"

"I know, but I didn't really get the picture until . . ." Bridge winced and rolled his eyes at himself. "Okay, so I don't always deal with reality either. Maybe it runs in the family."

Jamie did not smile.

Bridge sighed, then said what Jamie did not want to hear. "First thing tomorrow we'd better call your doctor and ask for a referral to a psychiatrist."

"Sure. Fine. Great. So they'll give her more pills and take her away and stick her in a hospital, and I'll never get her back." Her voice broke apart on the last few words.

"Hospitals aren't bad places," Bridge said quietly. Of course he would think that; he worked in one. "You're more likely to get her back that way than—"

"Shut up!" Jamie suddenly went a little crazy—maybe craziness did run in the family. She jumped to her feet, shouting at him. "Just shut up! She wouldn't be sick if it wasn't for you. I hate you!"

He did not shout back, but his voice sharpened as he said, "Look, that's not true. We don't know what made her the way she is."

"You made her worse!"

"She was sick before I came back. Did you expect me to sashay in here and make everything all right?"

She stared at him, remembering that yes, it was what she had hoped for. She also remembered that only a day earlier he had saved her butt at the risk of his life. What if there had been a knife in that mugger's pocket? Or a gun?

Bridger said more softly, "I never promised a happy ending. Nobody can promise that."

Nobody could promise anything. Grandma might never be herself again. She might never . . .

"Damn it, shut up," Jamie whispered, to herself, though Bridge might have thought she was talking to him. Damn everything, Grandma was going to be fine, and she, Jamie, was going to make it happen. She had to get herself moving and do something, that was all. Do something, fast, before they took Grandma away.

And she knew one thing she could do right that minute. She turned and strode the few steps to the kitchen phone.

"What are you doing?" Bridger and Kate both demanded at once.

She did not answer, but dialed information. Already knew the right area code.

"Chicago?" Her voice was only a little shaky. "Donald Duncan, please." She groped for pencil and paper.

Her knees were shakier than her voice. The Garibays had a wall phone, though, and she had to stand by it. The knees would just have to handle it.

Bridger sat silently, looking as tense as Jamie felt.

Jamie scrawled the number, then dialed. At the other end, a phone rang once . . . twice . . . three times. . . . Jamie had to remind herself to breathe.

Somebody picked up. "Hello?" said an older woman's throaty voice.

Please, God. "Hello, Amaryllis Duncan?"

"That's right."

Jamie could not believe it was so simple. She squeaked, "Lily Bridger's sister?"

"Yes!" The woman's voice went up almost as high as Jamie's. "Who is this?"

"Jamie."

"Jamie? Lily's Jamie? Oh, my God, Jamie, I have been trying to get news of you and her for *years*. Oh, my dear God." Aunt Mary was so excited, Jamie found herself actually smiling. "Are you okay?"

"Yeah." But that was an exaggeration, if not a downright lie. "Well," Jamie added, "Grandpa died." That was what had started everything.

There was a silence before Aunt Mary asked, "Who died?"

"Grandpa."

More silence. "Grandpa who?"

Was Aunt Amaryllis maybe a little dense? "Grandpa Bridger. Cletus. Grandma's husband. He's dead."

"Cletus is dead? When?"

"Three weeks ago."

"Was it—was he ill?"

"No. He just ate too much stewed chicken and had a heart attack."

Aunt Mary's voice had gone low. "How is your, um, how is Lily?"

Jamie admitted, "Not real good."

"No, I figured not," Aunt Mary said softly. "Jamie, where do you live? Give me your address and phone number this minute, honey, before I wet my pants."

She did not sound like the pants-wetting type, but the way she said it made Jamie smile again. She gave Aunt Mary the address, and the phone number, and Kate's phone number too. All the time she was wondering how to ask Aunt Mary the big question: Uh, would you happen to know, Aunt Mary, who my parents are? But she did not have to ask it over the phone. Aunt Mary took charge.

"I am coming down there," she said decisively. "I can hop in the car now and drive through the night and be there in the morning."

The idea of a sister of Grandma's who was able to hop

in a car and drive all night—apparently by herself—the idea took Jamie's breath away. She struggled to get words out. "You—you'll be here tomorrow morning?"

Listening, Bridger sat up straight, as if something had jabbed him.

Aunt Mary said politely, "If that's okay, Jamie."

"Yes! Of course, it's—it's wonderful."

"See you sometime tomorrow morning then, Jamie. And honey, don't fuss. And don't let Lily fuss. I don't need any special care and feeding, okay? I'd better go pack a few things. Bye, sweetie. See you soon."

Jamie hung up, leaned against the wall, and closed her eyes. When she opened them, Bridge was standing in front of her, watching her.

"You okay?"

"Yes, I'm *fine*!" she snapped at him.

He asked quietly, "You think Aunt Mary is going to help?"

Yes, damn it, that was what she wanted to believe. Jamie lifted her hands, grasping at air. But then she let them fall. "I don't know," she answered, her voice just as quiet as his. "I don't know what's going to happen."

"Neither do I," Bridge said.

The two of them looked at each other.

With his heart in his voice Bridge told her, "Jamie, all I want is what you want. I want Mama to be well."

Something snapped back into place in her head, and she knew it was true. He was not trying to take Grandma away from her. She swallowed hard, trying to make herself tell him she was sorry, but she didn't have to. He knew.

118

He stretched out his hand to her, and she ended up hugging him instead. Hanging onto him, really, with her head on his shoulder, but that was okay. Probably better than words.

Even though it was Sunday, Kate's mother had a meeting, and her father had been putting in extra time at the insurance office, trying to master the new computer system. It was late before they both got home. Next door, Mamaw was asleep—in her bed for a change, not on the closet floor, Kate knew. Bridger was on the sofa, because he did not want to sleep in what had been his father's room. Jamie was probably lying awake.

"It's bad over at Jamie's house," Kate told her parents.

Her mother gave her an inquiring look. Her father just yawned. "You should be in bed," he told her, wanting to go to bed himself.

"I need to talk with you two first. Jamie's in a real mess."

"Is this a ploy to try to keep us from moving?" Mr. Garibay inquired, more interested now.

"No. This is serious."

There was a lot Kate had not been telling them, partly because they were busy and she did not want to bother them, mostly because she had thought she could handle things herself. But now, sitting in the front room with the overhead light shining off her mother's perm and her father's bald spot, Kate told them everything. About Mamaw forgetting, Mamaw not eating, Mamaw in the closet. About Jamie's search ("She went to New York by her-

119

self?!" they both exclaimed.) and what she had found, and what remained unanswered. About Bridger's homecoming. About Mamaw again.

"Now it's like she's gone back in time. She's got her little boy back, and—and she's forgotten Jamie."

Kate's mother asked, "Do you mean really, or—"

"It's not an act. She's really forgotten. She looked at Jamie like she'd never seen her before in her life. She asked her where she was from, and where she went to school, and what grade she was in, and did she make good marks."

Mr. and Mrs. Garibay looked at each other. Mr. Garibay asked Kate, "What's being done?"

"Bridger is talking about getting her help, a psychiatrist. Jamie is scared."

Mr. Garibay nodded. He and Kate's mother looked at each other again. Then Kate's mother asked her, "What do you want us to do?"

Kate smiled, because she had known she could count on them. Her parents were good people. That was why they were so busy all the time, because they were the kind to do what they could for the community, and people kept them busy. But when Kate really needed them, there they were. They had listened to her without saying, You should have done such-and-so, or, Why didn't you tell us before? They wanted to help.

Kate told them what she had in mind, and the three of them stayed up until two A.M. talking it over.

Jamie could not sleep very well and got up early. But then all morning she just sat out on the front lawn, waiting for

Aunt Mary. She had her sketch pad, and time for her art at last, and even though the drawing was not going very well, it was better to be where she was than inside where Grandma was making potato salad and melon balls and a dessert called "heavenly hash" for lunch. Jamie had told her grandmother that Aunt Mary was coming, but Grandma seemed not to understand or hear her. When Bridger had told her, though, she had said, "Oh, how nice!" and started fixing goodies.

Normally Jamie would have helped. But she knew that Grandma would not let her help now. So Jamie was staying outside.

Kate came over and sat with her awhile, then had to go to school—it was the last day, only a half day really, but she still had to go. After Kate left, Bridger came outside once. "That's nice," he said, looking over Jamie's shoulder at the pencil portrait of a box turtle she was shading.

"Nice nothing. It stinks." She didn't want him to say complimentary, dishonest things when he knew better. He had seen the good pieces tacked to the walls of her room. He knew what she was capable of.

Bridger crouched down beside Jamie and looked at her as if assessing her private weather. She looked back.

"I'm okay," she told him, and it was almost true. "Go mix the cookie dough." She knew without going near the kitchen what Grandma had him doing.

He nodded. "I figure I better be with her while I can. It's not going to last." He went back in.

Around eleven, a white Ford Taurus station wagon roared up, and a woman who looked like a different version of Grandma got out: a stocky woman with a square face much like Grandma's, but with pewter-gray hair cut short and moussed into a stylish do. Aunt Mary wore elastic-waisted jeans, a Chicago Cubs T-shirt, and L.A. Gears. She moved as if she knew where she was going, and she was smiling as if she meant it.

"Jamie. You don't know me from Moses, but I'd know you anywhere. You poor dear, what happened to your face?" Without waiting to hear, she gave Jamie a huge hug. It felt good. At that point just being recognized and called by name felt good.

Jamie said to her husky shoulder, "Aunt Mary, there's a lot of things I have to ask you."

"I bet. But let me talk with Lily first." Aunt Mary patted Jamie, let go of her, and moved toward the house. Jamie followed.

Bridge met them at the kitchen door.

"Jamie!" Aunt Mary seemed not at all taken aback to use the same name as she strode in and bear-hugged him. "I didn't know you were going to be here! It's wonderful to see you, just wonderful."

Grandma turned, smiling, from the stove.

"Lily," Aunt Mary murmured, and her eyes went wet as she hugged her sister. "It's been so long, such a long, long time."

Grandma nodded agreement. "Since last Christmas, isn't it, Mary? Or was it the Christmas before?"

Aunt Mary stood back from her and peered at her. She said quietly, "Lil, it's been a good, solid ten years."

"Really? No. It can't be." Serenely Grandma shook her head. "It was Christmas a few years ago. We had

122

capon with sweet-pepper stuffing instead of turkey, remember? You brought the chowchow and the yams."

"That was back in Silver Valley."

Grandma blinked. "I beg your pardon?"

"That was quite awhile back," Aunt Mary said. "But we all lose track of time, don't we?" Her voice grew softer. "Lily, I'm so sorry to hear about Cletus."

"Cletus?" Grandma smiled a peaceful smile. "Oh, he's fine. He's over the flu now and back to work. He'll be home this evening."

Aunt Mary's face grew very still. Hesitant. Bridger and Jamie stood where they were. Nobody knew what to do or say.

Then Aunt Mary folded her arms. Jamie did not know which sister was older, Lily or Amaryllis—Aunt Mary looked a lot younger, yet the way she stood there with her L.A. Gears planted on the linoleum, she seemed like the elder. "Lily," she said firmly, "from what I hear, Cletus is dead. You didn't invite me to the funeral. You left Silver Valley and haven't been in touch all this time, Lily. Now, I want to know why."

Grandma's eyes widened in shock—how could Mary say such crazy things?—but then she blinked and turned away from the question. "Jamie, set the table please, sweetie," she said to Bridger. "Mary, why don't you have a seat. How are Don and the children?" Amaryllis was being difficult, Grandma seemed to be thinking, and she had to smooth things over. If she could get lunch on the table quickly, everything would be okay. Nobody would make unpleasant conversation over lunch. Grandma hurried to the refrigerator and brought out potato salad,

123

lunch meat, sliced cheese, sandwich rolls. Her arms were getting loaded. Automatically Jamie went to help.

Jamie walked to Grandma and stretched out her hands to take something. But Grandma stared at Jamie and put the food on the countertop instead of handing it to her. Grandma said politely, "You, ah, young lady—I can never remember your name—are you staying for lunch?"

To Jamie it was like getting punched in the stomach. She felt sick. She could not answer.

Aunt Mary burst out, "Lil, that's Jamie! What's the matter with you?"

Grandma gave her sister a quelling look. "Amaryllis, you're confused. *That's* my Jamie." She pointed to her son, who had set down the luncheon plates and had come over to stand close to the "young lady," touching her shoulder to let her know he was there.

Sitting at the table, Aunt Mary said tartly, "Lil, I never have understood why you named them both the same, but it's a free country, and I suppose a person can name their children what they want."

Jamie felt her heart stop. She heard Bridger gasp, and he clutched at her shoulder.

Aunt Mary said sternly to her sister, "Now you may be able to get away with this 'Grandma' nonsense around here, but you can't with me. I was there, and I know what's what. I know little Jamie is your daughter, just the same as big Jamie is your son."

Grandma began to wail deep in her throat, but for once Jamie did not care. She was gawking at Bridger, and his eyes, gazing back at her, were alight like blue windows with candles in them.

He whispered, "I—I have a sister? A kid sister?"

"You're my—brother?"

Bright wings and black wings were whirling and whirling in Jamie's mind, and she did not know whether they were vultures or God-sized butterflies. No, she had no father, and her mother—her mother was a crazy woman who had lied to her—but yes, yes, she had Bridge, the other Jamie Bridger, her very own brother—butterflies and joy took over. Jamie screamed and jumped up and down with joy, and she kept jumping while Bridge grabbed her and danced her around the kitchen, both of them laughing and crying and flinging back their heads and shouting at the ceiling.

"I've got a big brother!"

"Sister! I've got a sister!"

"Yo, Bro!" Jamie yelled at him.

"Yo, Sis!" He spun her around and lifted her up off the linoleum and bear-hugged her.

Wailing, Grandma hid her face behind her wrinkled hands. Aunt Mary got up and went to her. "Lily, what's the matter? It's all right."

But Grandma seemed not to hear. "Daddy would not approve," she whimpered.

"Lil—"

"Daddy would not approve!" Grandma screamed, and she scuttled blindly out of the room. Jamie heard the panicky, faltering footsteps heading up the stairs, and knew without having to look: Grandma was going back into her dark hole again, back to hiding in the closet.

Chapter

11

⌒

"They had you to replace me," Bridge said. He was sitting at the kitchen table, looking dazed, giddy with revelation. "I swear to God, that is just what they did. Separate bedrooms for sixteen years, and then I don't turn out the way they want, so pop, they get together and make you, Jamie."

"Except I turned out to be a girl," Jamie said. "I always had the feeling I wasn't what he wanted. Grandpa, I mean." She winced. He was not her grandpa—he was her father. But she did not want to call him that. "Um, Cletus."

Bridge said happily, "Pooh on him. I bet Ma loved having a girl."

Jamie had to smile. "I think she kind of did." She stopped smiling. "But if I was supposed to replace you, that kind of explains what's going on with her, right? She's got it in her head that only one Jamie Bridger is allowed."

⌒

Bridge sighed and said, "She's in need of help, Jamie. She's ill. Cletus was sick, the marriage was sick. I never realized before how strange and sick my parents were."

Jamie nodded. Like her, he had gotten used to what he was raised with. He had accepted the way his parents were without thinking about it much until he had to.

"I feel stupid." Bridger started to grin again. "David says he was betting all along we were brother and sister, only he didn't want to say it." Bridge had called David to share the good news. "But I swear, it never ever occurred to me. I just never dreamed Ma and Pa would do that. They seemed like they hadn't had a sexual thought in years."

"About thirty years," Jamie agreed.

"I don't remember ever seeing him kiss her, not even on the cheek."

Aunt Mary came in, sighing. She had been upstairs trying one last time to talk Lily out of the closet. "No use," she muttered.

"Aunt Mary," Jamie appealed to her, "are you absolutely sure I'm Grandma's daughter?" Hearing what she had just said, she flinched.

"Lily's daughter?" Aunt Mary smiled the wide, sweet smile that definitely came from Grandma's side of the family, not Grandpa's. "Yes, honey child, I'm sure. She stayed with me while she was pregnant with you. I was there when you were born."

"You *were?*" Jamie's heart stopped, then thumped as if it wanted to get out of her chest and dance. She had never known until that moment how much she had missed having a history, an account of her own birth.

127

"Yes, indeed. At Chicago General." Aunt Mary sat down, pushing the potato salad out of her way. Nobody wanted lunch.

In a hushed voice Jamie asked, "When was I born? In the middle of the night?"

"Five in the morning. Just in time for a summer sunrise." Aunt Mary contemplated Jamie with wise warm eyes. "You were kind of purple and fuzzy, like a big bayberry, and absolutely beautiful."

Jamie had never felt so real. She sat stunned by her own validity. Across the table, Bridger was leaning back and laughing at the look on her face.

Aunt Mary patted Jamie's hand. "We both just adored you," she said. "I cried when she went home and took you away."

"But—" This was all very odd. "But why was she staying with you? Was Grand—uh, was Cletus there?"

"No, he wasn't. He was in Silver Valley. Lil didn't ever really tell me what was going on." Aunt Mary frowned into the distance, thinking about that time. "Trouble with Cletus, I figured." Her gaze shifted to Bridger. "I knew you had gone away, Jamie."

"Bridge," he said. "Call me Bridge. 'Jamie' is kind of effeminate for a good-looking young man like me, don't you think?" He was giving her a wry smile, trying to tell her something. Aunt Mary gave him a level gaze in return.

"Bridge, they never explained what happened, and I guess it's none of my business. . . ."

"I fell in love. With a guy," Bridge told her quietly. "Pa found out."

Aunt Mary sighed. There was silence for a moment.

128

Then Aunt Mary said, "Honey, I wish you had come to me."

Bridge ducked his head, embarrassed by his own emotions, trying to hide. "I'm all right," he mumbled.

"Now you are," Mary said. "Back then it must have been very hard."

Bridger got his wry smile back and looked up. "I was the talk of the town," he said. "Ma was ashamed, I guess. Needed to get away."

"That's what I thought then." Aunt Mary shook her head. "But it's not what I think now. Or, it's not the whole story. I think Cletus was ashamed—of having a pregnant wife. I think he did not want her to be seen." She looked at Jamie. "I think he was already planning to pass you off as somebody else's."

For years there had been an imaginary father for Jamie, maybe young, maybe cute, maybe a nice guy who just did not know about her. Now there was a real father who was old, and hard, and—embarrassed that she was born? It was enough to make a person crazy. Jamie said fiercely, "I hate him. I'm glad he's dead."

Aunt Mary said, "Now, it's not all his fault. He was not always a terrible person. Lily helped make him that way." Jamie gawked, Bridge looked blank, and Mary smiled sadly at the two of them. "She gave him too much," she explained. "She handed her whole life to him on a platter; how was he not supposed to become a dictator? Don't ever do that, Jamie. It's wonderful to fall in love, but don't give away your soul."

Jamie sat staring. Upstairs there was an old woman cringing in a dark hiding place, and for the first time

Grandma's sickness was making sense to Jamie. Grandma had given her selfhood to Grandpa, and now that he was dead, it was gone. Resurrection Lily Lutz Bridger did not know who she was anymore.

But how did anybody know that, ever? What was selfhood? How old did a person need to be to have it?

Who am I? Who was Jamie Bridger?

She knew who her parents were now. Why did it not seem like an answer?

"Aunt Mary." Maybe thinking similar thoughts, Bridge asked, "What was Ma like, really? Before?"

So Amaryllis sat in the afternoon sunshine that slanted through the kitchen windows, and she told them about her sister.

Lily was like a kitchen-garden flower: sweet, a little bit homely, shy, but as with many shy people, when she actually said something it was usually worth listening to. She had intelligence; she did well in school. But their father did not believe in college for women. Lily stayed home, and cooked for her father after her mother died, and thought about things—the Cold War, the atom bomb, fallout shelters, children starving in India. She did not go out much but seemed always to be watching the world for answers. She did not date but seemed to be waiting. For ten years she waited.

Then Cletus Bridger came to town. He was a bit older than she was, but handsome, intense, alive with sureness. "What they call, these days, charismatic," Amaryllis said. A tent preacher, he had convictions about what was wrong with a world that contained Khrushchev and Elvis, and the courage to speak his mind. Lily went to hear him, and he seemed to her to be the answer, the man she had been waiting for.

"And I don't think she ever changed her mind about that."

Shy though she was, she went up to him afterward to talk. He came home with her to talk. He came back the next day. She was lost in adoration of him. He saw it and smiled on her. He stayed in town longer than he had planned. They spent a lot of time together.

"She was twenty-nine," Amaryllis said, smiling. "He was thirty-three. They took a lot of teasing, especially from me. I was always the mouthy one, and I had been married eight years already and figured I knew everything, and— oh, well, it wasn't just me. The whole family got a kick out of them. The whole town did. Poor Lily. She and her beau would go for a walk, and when they got back, half a dozen people would be waiting to quiz them about where they'd been and what they'd done. Lily would just blush like a rose. But Cletus wouldn't blush." Aunt Mary stopped smiling. "He would get mad."

"And go ballistic," Bridge said, wry again, as if his father's rages were not unfamiliar to him.

"Yeppers. He would fly right off the handle. Anybody else would have just teased back, but there he would be, yelling and screaming about how his feelings for Lily were pure and chaste. She was a spotless angel. Their converse was the converse of kindred spirits. How dare we have such dirty minds. Sex was a dirty thing to him." Aunt Mary stopped talking and looked thoughtfully at Bridger.

He grinned at her. "I figured it out years ago," he told

131

her. "Dates don't lie. I was born about six months after they were married, right?"

"Very premature," Amaryllis said dryly.

"I guess it was a scandal."

"Back then it could have been, but we all loved Lily. And we would have liked Cletus just for being human, if he'd let us."

But being human was not what Cletus Bridger wanted. The birth of his son, proof that he was not above human failings, chagrined him. He felt shamed into giving up his ministry and taking a secular job. He changed. Striving to make up for his lapse, ever more intent on the exemplary life, he frowned through his days, becoming dour and strict with Lily and the boy. The woman had led him astray. The boy reflected on him. In his dealings with them, Cletus needed to feel completely in control.

"You're lucky you're a girl, Jamie," Bridger told her. "He probably left you mostly to Ma. But me, he was always on my back."

Ultimately, however, even Cletus Bridger could not control his growing son. And when he could no longer control him, he cut him off. Like a wrong thought, an unacceptable impulse, an evil lurking in the heart, the bad boy had to be thoroughly rejected. After casting him out, Cletus led Lily in going through the house, gathering up everything that had belonged to their son, taking it all to the dump. When all traces of the youngster were erased, Cletus ordered Lily to forget she had ever had a son. And, being Lily, she set about doing so. If she cried in the night, she tried not to let Cletus know.

He gave her another child. This time the two of them

132

were going to do it right. This time the child would grow to be a credit to Bridger righteousness.

But almost as soon as it was accomplished, Cletus began to be afraid. Had he fallen into shame again? His wife was forty-six years old, he was fifty, and soon the whole world would see her condition and know what lewd act the two of them had been committing.

"He told me my parents were evil people," Jamie said, her voice soft with not wanting to believe it. "Filthy, lewd, evil people. He called them a slut and a goat. He shouted it. Did he—was he talking about himself? Was he talking about . . ." She didn't want to call her Grandma. "Was he talking about his own wife?"

Nobody wanted to answer.

"He was crazy," Jamie whispered, hot with hatred of him. "He drove her crazy."

"But she went along with him." Aunt Mary shook her head. "Everybody should learn to stand up for themselves, but she never stood up to him about anything. When we lost our father, she started calling Cletus 'Daddy.' And she obeyed him as if she had no mind of her own."

He sent her away to keep her pregnancy from being talked about in Silver Valley. When she had the baby, it was a girl instead of the expected boy. They named it "Jamie" as planned, but Cletus knew in his heart that the wrong-gender child was a reproach to him, like the boy that had turned out wrong, a judgment for having committed a carnal act. Therefore, so that the world would continue to perceive him as a righteous man, the child had to be hidden. Back in Silver Valley he instructed Lily to pass the child off as a visiting niece, a little girl she baby-sat, a neighbor's child, or to keep her out of sight altogether. But Lily was dangerously softhearted about the girl. Around the house she permitted her to call her Mama. And the relatives knew. Lily's family in particular knew and teased unmercifully.

"Especially me," Aunt Mary admitted. "I simply could not stop. I could not believe any man could be so strait-laced. I kept trying and trying to make him laugh. And then the older you grew, Jamie, the more you looked like him."

"Oh, no." Bridge got the picture and groaned.

"Oh, yes. By the time she was three or four, they couldn't pass her off as the neighbor's kid anymore. I kept teasing Cletus, asking him, when she started school and he had to fill out the papers, was he finally going to admit to her?"

"No way," Jamie said bitterly. "It was easier to move. Run away from everybody. Lie to me. Tell me they were my grandma and grandpa so I wouldn't embarrass them by being their daughter."

Silence. Then Bridger stretched out his hand to her and said softly, "We were all victims of an obsession, Jamie. Even Pa."

"Silly man," Aunt Mary grumbled. "He missed out on so much. Jamie, if you were mine, I would have been dancing in the delivery room."

Jamie gave up her bitterness and laughed, thinking suddenly of Shirley and her dancing turtles. Imagine Aunt Mary doing a fandango on the birthing table.

"You know," Aunt Mary said thoughtfully, "Lily is too young to be so old. You know, she's younger than I am, and I don't consider myself an old woman. I might live to be a hundred, if I take after the Lutz women. So might she. There might be lots of years left for Lily. Do you think it's too much to ask, after all she's been through, that they should be good years?"

"Asking's got nothing to do with it," said Bridger, standing up. "We're going to make it happen." He headed for the phone to call the doctor.

Chapter

12

Bridger waited until Aunt Mary and Jamie were in the car, out the driveway, down the street, and out of sight before he moved from the window. Aunt Mary had wanted to find a mall (there weren't any within thirty miles) and take Jamie clothes shopping, but Jamie had asked if they couldn't just go hiking in the state park instead. Trees and birds and such seemed to mean something to Jamie. Comfort her. And Jamie needed comforting.

Bridger sighed. Jamie was having a hard time, and he knew how she felt, how it felt to be a kid with your world changing, out of control, with the people you love failing you.

He turned away from the window and trudged up the stairs.

In the center of the dark bedroom he stood still. "Ma?"

No answer.

Bridger decided it was okay to try something. He knew he could get her out of there—sometimes at the hospital where he worked he had to lift patients twice his size. But he did not want to manhandle his mother unless he absolutely had to.

In a deep, commanding tone he said, "Lily."

"Daddy?" His mother's voice came to him like a black moth across the darkness, wavering.

"No," Bridge said, "it's me." Let her decide who "me" was. At least he had not lied to her.

"Daddy?"

"Come out of there," he told her.

Coat hangers rattled. Lily wobbled out of the closet and stood staring at him.

"Come on." He beckoned, keeping his voice carefully neutral. "It's time for your appointment."

She looked puzzled. But evidently he was a family male of some sort—a daddy, and it did not much matter which one exactly—so she obeyed him. She followed him downstairs. "My purse," she said, and she picked it up. "Do I look okay?" She patted at her braids, which were coming loose; she had not let Jamie fix them for her.

"You look fine." Bridger almost said Ma, but caught himself in time.

Mrs. Leweski's old Buick, borrowed for a couple of hours, was parked out front. Lily followed him to it. He opened the passenger door for her.

For just about twenty hours, less than a full day, he had had his mother back. Now here stood a woman, almost a stranger, with the round eyes of a child. His mother was gone.

Too bad, Bridge. Grow up. Toughen up.

Maybe the mother he wanted back had never really existed. Memories tended to deceive. Maybe she lived only in his dreams.

Just the same, before the old woman with the unraveling braids got in the car, he stopped her a moment, put his arms around her sloping shoulders, and hugged her.

"Did you have to drag her?" Jamie asked afterward.

"No." Bridge shook his head. "She went on her own."

Jamie sat in Grandma's armchair, studying its upholstery, tracing a fleur-de-lis with her fingertip. "Did she cry or anything?"

Bridge shook his head. Jamie tried to think of what questions she really needed to ask, tried to imagine what a psychiatric ward was like. Would there be anyplace for Grandma to hide?

"It would be better if she did cry," Bridge said in a low voice. He sat straddling a ladder-back chair pulled in from the kitchen, his chin resting on its wooden top rung. "The ones who scream and cry, they hit bottom faster, and then they bounce back and get well faster. Somebody passive like Ma—it's going to take a while."

Jamie's glance shot up to catch on him. "How long?"

He looked back at her but did not answer. The shadows in his eyes were answer enough.

"Does Lily seem to understand at all what's happening?" Aunt Mary asked. She sat on the bottom step of the stairs. Nobody wanted to sit in the recliner.

"Not really. She's confused." Bridge straightened and turned to face her. "But that could be good, Aunt Mary.

138

Being confused, it's like a chance to rearrange the furniture, you know?"

"Maybe she'll start thinking for herself again, you mean? I hope so."

"That's one of the reasons for getting her out of here. New surroundings, new thoughts." Bridge turned to Jamie. "Did you know the very best facility in the state is in Silver Valley? As soon as I can arrange it, I want to get her transferred there. They have a model outpatient program, and Ma's a good candidate. She's no danger to herself or anybody else. If the doctors agree, once her medication's adjusted we can find her a place to stay in town."

Jamie sat silent, not looking at him. She felt very tired, and kind of numb.

"Jamie?"

She did not have to answer, because there was a knock at the door. Without waiting for someone to get up, Kate came in.

"Hey, Katie!" Bridge greeted her.

"Hi." Kate grinned at him. She had heard he was Jamie's brother and had performed an impromptu dance of joy on the front lawn. "Hello, Aunt Mary." She had met Aunt Mary, who of course was not her aunt, but who cared. "Jamie." Kate came over and sat on the arm of Jamie's chair. Grandpa never would have allowed that. Do it all the time, and it would damage the chair. Smile all the time, and you would probably damage your face.

"I saw you took Mamaw out in the car," Kate said to Bridge.

He knew what she was really asking. "Yes. She's in the hospital for a while."

139

Kate nodded, unsurprised. "They can take care of her better than Jamie and me."

"And let you two get on with living. Yes."

"I can send her a card or some flowers."

"She'd like that."

Kate swiveled to look at Jamie. It was a serious Kate look. "Listen, Jame, I didn't get a chance to tell you before, I was kind of waiting for the parents to get home and come over here with me, but they said go ahead because you might be worrying." What was Kate all wound up about, just when Jamie felt too bone-tired to deal with anything? "Listen, what it is is this: If you need a place to go, you're supposed to come stay with Mom and Dad and me."

Jamie tried to connect with what Kate was telling her. It did not work, but she knew she ought to say something. "Um, thanks," she mumbled, "but I'd just be in the way when you have to get ready to move."

"No, doofus, you would move with us!" Kate hopped off the armchair and hunkered down by Jamie, earnest. "We talked it over, and we want you to come along with us. Stay with us for as long as you need to. Be family. You'll love the pond, and the woods, and—heck, it's not just for you. It's for me too." Kate's voice went husky. "So I don't have to leave my sister behind."

Jamie sat and could not think what to say.

"You don't have to answer right away." Kate bounced up and gave Jamie one of her fierce, quick hugs. "Think about it." She was out the door again like a feather on the wind.

"Jamie?" Bridge asked again.

140

She did not look at him, did not answer.

Aunt Mary spoke up. "You know I want you to come home with me, Jamie," she said in her forthright way. "Stick to real family. You have your uncle Don and all your cousins to meet."

"Or come back with me," Bridge said.

She jerked her head up to look at him.

"I have to leave tomorrow," he told her. "Gotta be back on the job Wednesday."

She felt shock jolting her eyes wide open.

"There's plenty of room," Aunt Mary was saying as if nothing had interrupted. "Your pick of spare bedrooms since all the kids are grown. I know your uncle Don would enjoy having you around. It gets really dull for him, being home with his oxygen tank all the time."

Tomorrow. Bridge was leaving tomorrow.

He was looking at her. "I know you're a nature girl," he said, "but think of this: New York is the art capital of the world. Museums. Special high schools just for artists."

Jamie sat woodenly.

"Sleep on it," Bridge said gently. "You don't have to decide what to do till morning."

Jamie began to understand why Grandma had started hiding in the closet. If you did that, it was as if you could stop the world, stop time. Keep the room dark enough, and morning might never come.

About two A.M., wide awake, chest aching, Jamie could not stand it any longer and got up. Barefoot, in her oldest Bambi-print cotton pajamas, she padded downstairs.

She could see him, her brother, the colors of milk and

141

honey in the streetlamp light, lying on the sofa in a T-shirt and running shorts, sound asleep. People always looked so beautiful, so much like angels, when they were sleeping. At least Bridger did.

"Bridge," she whispered. She touched his arm.

He turned his head groggily toward her. She kneeled beside him.

"Please don't go," she begged him.

He looked back at her, unblinking, not surprised to see her there. But maybe nurses were used to being awakened by crying people in the middle of the night.

"Please stay with me." Tears were running down her face, making the room swim, her voice turn watery.

"Can't, Jamie," he said, matter-of-fact. "I'll lose my job."

"Get a job here."

"I thought of that." Bridger swung his legs over the edge of the sofa and sat up to talk with her. "But the kind of work David does, he has to live in the city."

She stared, barely able to see him through tears. David? "But I'm your sister!" How could he put David ahead of her?

He hesitated. Maybe she could win. She had to win.

"Yes, you sure are," he said softly, seriously.

She was going to win. "Well, then—"

"And David's my lover."

"But—"

In a low, taut voice Bridge said to her, "You and David are the two most important things that have ever happened to me. Don't make me choose between the two of you, Jamie. Please."

"But, Bridge—"

"Sis," Bridge appealed, "he's special. He—he's the one, don't you see? Don't you know what I'm talking about? Haven't you dreamed of finding somebody to love?"

Damn, yes she had, and she could not take that away from him. It was no use, it was no use, she had to let him go, and she could not bear it. Jamie put her head down on the sofa and bawled.

She felt Bridge's hands settle warm on her shoulders, like two nesting doves. "Jamie," he said not quite steadily, "I wish I could save you from all the pain, but I can't. One thing I've found out, you can't save anybody from anything till you save yourself."

"I don't want to go live with Aunt Mary," Jamie sobbed. "I don't even want to live with Kate. Or you, if I'm gonna—be in your way." Giving up the fight, crying, Jamie found that she had reached truth. "I just want things to stop changing, that's all! I want—Grandma back."

Bridge sat very still with his hands on her shoulders for a moment. Then he said, "C'mere," and tugged gently at her arms. He pulled her up to sit on the sofa beside him. Then he slipped one hand under her knees, the other behind her back, and he lifted her as if she were a three-year-old. Lord, he was strong. Jamie found herself sitting in his lap, nestled in his arms like a little kid, with her head against his shoulder.

He murmured, "Of course you want her back. You've been fighting like a Comanche for weeks to get her back.

You went out to capture a miracle, and all you got was me."

The words made Jamie's chest hurt like fire. She hid her face against him and sobbed.

Bridge laid his cheek against her hair. "Okay," he said, low, close to her ear, "okay, let's say just for right now I'm what you wanted. I'm the daddy, the big strong daddy and you're just a poor little kid, right? And I'm gonna take care of you. How does it feel?"

Jamie pressed close to the warmth of his broad chest. The warmth, and the steadiness of his arms around her, helped her stop crying, helped her breathing calm down. She kept her eyes closed and held still.

"How does it feel?"

"Good," Jamie whispered.

He smiled. She felt his smile against her hair. He kept holding her, and softly he began to rock her in his arms.

Jamie nestled against him and let him cuddle her. He didn't say anything, just held her and rocked and hummed deep in his chest like a big cat. Monotonous. Like she was supposed to go to sleep. Jamie was not sleepy, but she began to feel hot. No longer comfortable, no longer in need of comforting. Poor little kid? She was not a little kid anymore. More like a big kid, too big for this. Sitting on Bridger's lap and hanging onto him made her feel bent over, crowded, cramped. She pushed herself away from him and sat up.

He stopped rocking and humming and gave her a quizzical smile. "How does it feel?" he asked again.

"I'm beginning to feel a little bit stupid," Jamie admitted.

144

"Good. Get off. Ow. My legs hurt." Bridger grimaced as she got up, then jiggled his legs and rubbed them hard with his hands. "Lord. Next time I'll sit on your lap, okay?"

Next time. She had to smile.

"God, you're solid. You take a couple of boxing lessons and you could beat me up, you know that?"

Jamie rolled her eyes and sat on the floor.

"You okay now?"

"Yeah." She sighed, mostly with relief. Somehow things had sorted themselves out in her head, and she found she had made her decision. "I'll go stay with Kate." It was not a hard choice, really. Like Kate had said—they were already sisters.

Bridge nodded, watching her. "It's not such a bad deal," he remarked, "having people practically fighting over who gets you."

"I know. I really like Aunt Mary. It's just—Uncle Don's emphysema—I don't want to go live where somebody is getting ready to die. I'm sorry, but I just don't. I've about had it with dying and stuff."

Bridger nodded, and she remembered what he had said about needing to save yourself first. It was okay.

"And you and—and David. . . ." She picked at the carpet as she talked. "The art schools and everything sound nice, but—maybe when I'm older. I'm not sure I could take New York for long. Sometimes I really need to walk in the woods."

This was true, but it was also true that the apartment was small, and Bridge and David were still working things out, and—she wanted Bridge to be happy.

Maybe he even knew it. He said softly, "Jamie, you are thoroughly wonderful."

Startled, she stopped picking at the carpet and looked up at him.

He said, "It's not like we'll be strangers. I'll be visiting, and I'm gonna want you to visit me, and I'm gonna be calling you all the time, but do you know why? Ask me if you're a poor little thing."

The way he said it was so funny, she had to grin.

"Ask me if I feel sorry for my kid sister."

"Do you feel sorry for your kid sister?"

Quietly, intensely, he told her, "I don't have to. Jamie, you're gonna be fine. I don't have to be a nice guy and take care of you. If I hang around, it's because I love you."

Chapter

13

September. The longest, strangest summer of Jamie's life was behind her, and she was living in a new place, going to a new school, thinking some new thoughts. She had her hair cut short, wild and wavy on top, and it looked great. She had her ears pierced. It was Friday, a bright blue-and-gold Friday, and Jamie watched for red-tailed hawks in the sky as Mom Garibay drove her down to Silver Valley to visit. It was only about forty minutes to Silver Valley from where Jamie and the Garibays lived now, so almost anytime Jamie wanted, she could go spend the weekend.

The car pulled in at the gingerbreaded house on Sweet Gum Lane. Jamie jumped out, grabbed her suitcase and her sketch pad, kissed Mom G., and ran to find Shirley.

There were voices out back. Jamie left her stuff on the porch and headed around the side of the house.

"Hello, Jamie!" Shirley called the minute Jamie came around the corner. Shirley, grinning toothily. Shirley, sitting on the back stoop, a turtle in her lap, with Mamaw sitting beside her.

"Hello, dear," Mamaw greeted Jamie.

Seeing doctors nearly every day had not yet helped Lily Bridger accept that Jamie was her daughter. She treated her as a family friend, a tiny bit more warmly each time she saw her, and that was okay. Jamie did not know if she would ever be able to call Lily "Mama" anyway, after the way Lily had lied to her, passing her off as a grandchild for so long. But she did not want to call her Grandma anymore, so she called her Mamaw, the way Kate did.

"Hi, Mamaw." Jamie checked to make sure there were no turtles in the way, then vaulted the fence and walked up to Shirley and Lily. She hugged them both at once. "Giving the guys a touch-up, I see." Mamaw had a turtle in her lap too, and both she and Shirley were wielding fine-pointed paintbrushes. Mamaw appeared to be in the process of painting her turtle's toenails enamel red.

"This is not a guy," Mamaw said coyly. "This is Lola. A girl. And a girl gets to be dolled up a bit." Lola lazed in Mamaw's lap with her head out, observing her manicure. Lola had rosebuds painted on her shell, and her name in gold script. Lola was dolled up.

"Very stylish," Jamie said. Lola hissed at her.

"Lola," Mamaw rebuked, "be nice."

Shirley said eagerly, "Jamie, come inside. See what else your Mamaw's been doing." She put her brush in water, set down her turtle (it was Sam), jumped up, and beckoned.

Jamie followed her into the house. In the kitchen and

dining room things looked the same, but in the living room—Jamie saw and let out a yell, then stood and laughed. A huge Crayola box squatted in the middle of the floor, and every sheep in the wallpaper was brightly crayoned a different color.

Jamie jumped and clapped her hands, laughing.

"Your Mamaw started it," Shirley declared, all innocence. "I just happened to buy the crayons one day."

"You two nuts! Tell the truth, did you do it or did she?"

"We both did! We had such fun. But that's not what I meant to show you. Come on upstairs." Shirley trotted up the steps and stopped at the door of Mamaw's bedroom, the big back bedroom. Right behind her, Jamie looked past her and gasped.

The room was full of light. Somebody had taken the drapes off the windows to let in more light. The bed was pushed over to one side, and amid all the light stood an easel, and on the easel was a half-finished painting depicting a winged hand stitching together a field of bright wildflowers into a crazy quilt to cover a mountain's knees. More paintings leaned against the walls: a broken vase with its flowers spilling; a brown-braided, square-faced girl with blue cornflowers instead of eyes; a field of white cloud-flowers growing down from the sky.

"Mamaw did these?" Jamie exclaimed. It was hard to believe. They were good in a way. The paint was applied strongly, as if by a sure hand.

"Yes! I guess we know now where your artistic talent comes from, Jamie."

"But I never even knew she could draw!"

149

"She's going to be surprising you from now on. She's starting to come out of her shell." Shirley walked to a window and looked down at Mamaw sitting on the stoop, Mamaw painting fuchsia scallops on the edge of Lola's carapace. "I can't tell you—she's never been any trouble, of course, and I'm so glad you talked me into boarding her here, Jamie—but now that she's starting to take an interest, she's a delight to have around. She's just a delight."

Jamie stared at Mamaw's paintings. They were very strange, maybe not the work of a normal person, but she liked them. They were quirky, full of life. Seeing them was like meeting someone interesting she had never known.

"Did Bridge get here yet? Has he seen these?"

"Yes, he loved them. He should be back any minute. Went to have a late lunch with Ian Russell."

"I hear him!" There were footsteps on the porch. Jamie ran downstairs and reached the front door just as Bridge opened it.

"Hey, Sis!" He bear-hugged her. "Ian says hi."

"Hi to her too. How's David?"

"Good." He gave her a soft smile. "It's good, Jamie."

He seemed relaxed and happy, as if he was starting to feel at home in Silver Valley again, not tense the way he had been the first few times he had come back here, not spooked the way he had been seeing this house again.

The house seemed to help Mamaw. It connected her with a happier time. Eventually it might connect her with the bad memories too.

There she stood in the kitchen doorway peering at Bridger. As if he had just come in from playing outside

150

she said to him, "Jamie, honey, you should wear your jacket. It's starting to get cold. How was school?"

He shrugged and turned to Jamie. "How *was* school?"

"Fine." She liked her new school, which had a can-do attitude. It had not been necessary for her to repeat a grade after all, just make up some missed work. Jamie said to her mother, "Mamaw, I like your flowers."

"Flowers?"

"Your paintings."

Mamaw blinked, uncomprehending. Her boy was here, so her flower paintings did not exist. "Supper?" she courted Bridger, though usually Mamaw did not cook anymore. "What would you like for supper?"

"Ma, I just ate!"

"I'm hungry," Jamie said, and for just an instant Mamaw looked at her with what might have been recognition before she turned away and smiled on her son again.

Sleeping that night in the front bedroom, the one with the peach-colored wallpaper, Jamie dreamed of turtles rising like angels out of their shells and dancing across fields of flowers.

She got up the moment she awoke. On a sunny Saturday morning, who could stay in bed? It was really early, though, barely past dawn. Even Shirley was not up yet. And of course Mamaw was still asleep. Her medicine made her sleep a lot.

Early though it was, Bridger was dressed and outside already. Jamie spotted him from the bathroom window. He was wandering around at the bottom of the yard, looking at the grass, the sky, hunkering down to converse with the turtles.

Jamie dressed fast, ran downstairs and headed out there, treading carefully to make sure she didn't step on Otto or Suzy or anybody. "Morning!" she sang to Bridger, unnecessarily. Of course it was morning. It was about as morning as it gets. Heady air. Glowing rosy sky.

"Hey, Sis." He gave her his wide, warm smile. "Whatcha doing up so early?"

"You should talk. What are you doing?"

"Nothing." But Jamie could tell he had something on his mind. He seemed restless, full of energy. Pacing from turtle to turtle, tree to tree.

"Ma seems better," he said.

In a sunny-morning mood Jamie did not really feel like talking about Mamaw. She was thinking that she should have brought her sketch pad out with her. But the way Bridge was prowling around the yard—maybe he needed to talk.

"I can't believe those paintings she did," he called to Jamie.

"Yeah. They're good."

"She's stretching toward the light," Bridge said.

"Huh?"

"She's growing. Changing." Bridge stood still a minute to look at Jamie. "Why don't you call her Ma, Sis? It might help her face that she's your mother."

Jamie sighed, but had to admit it was a valid question. Okay, it looked as if she and Bridge were going to use the morning solitude to have a serious conversation. She thought before she answered. "Partly, I'm still mad at her." Being told a lifelong whopper of a lie can reasonably have that effect on a person.

Bridge stepped closer, looked at her and nodded, unsurprised. "You planning to forgive her eventually?"

"I guess." Jamie thought some more. "Mostly, I just can't get used to it," she admitted. "Like, Mamaw being my mother—that's scary. What if I turn out like her?"

Bridger's eyes crinkled as he smiled. "As in, a wonderful cook? As in, big and old and cushy?"

"As in, crazy! What if I get mental when I turn thirty?"

Bridger walked over and leaned against the fence beside her, giving her his full attention. "Why would you?"

"People say girls always grow up to be just like their mothers."

"Bull."

"Well, isn't mental illness hereditary?"

"Not what she has. Jamie, listen." Bridge turned toward her, stretching out his hand to her. "No way are you going to end up like Ma, because you're a lot tougher than she's ever been. Look at the way you took hold after Pa died. Look at the way you fought back when that son of a bitch was beating you around, the first time I saw you." His voice went husky with emotion. "Look at the way you moved heaven and earth to find me."

Jamie blinked, for a moment seeing herself the way another person did: She was strong, a fighter, a person who got things done? Then the doubts took hold again. "Maybe Mamaw was braver too, when she was younger."

"Maybe a little, but I doubt she was like you, Jamie. I see the old man in you."

"Thanks a *lot!*" Jamie still remembered Grandpa—no, her father—with loathing.

"What's so bad? That's not bad. Remember, he was smart, and tough, and he did what he decided to do. The bad things about him you can leave behind. You don't have to be just like him. I'm his son; am I just like him?"

"Noooo, not hardly."

Bridger couldn't have been less like Grandpa. Easy to talk with. Funny, the more they talked the more they had to say. And Jamie talked with Bridger a lot. He had been phoning her every few days since he had known her, and she called him almost as much as he called her, and they saw each other at least once a month at Shirley's, and Jamie was going to New York to visit him around Christmastime. If Kate was her best friend and sister, then Bridge was her other best friend and brother. She was lucky to have found him. Bridge was so special. There were things he understood without saying, and other things she could tell only to him in the whole world.

One of which was on her mind this very minute, as he stood there running a fingernail along the fence wire.

"Bridge . . ."

He looked up at her. "What?"

The thing about having family was . . . No, she couldn't say it. "Never mind."

He stopped making fence music, stood up straight, and looked at her. "Never mind what?"

No. He might be hurt, he might get angry and never forgive her. "Nothing."

"Jamie, c'mon." He stood watching her—somehow he

knew it was important. "Tell me. I'm your brother. What's the matter?"

He *was* her brother. That was kind of the problem. But he was her brother, so he had to forgive her. Quickly, before she lost her nerve, Jamie blurted it out. "What if I'm gay?"

"What? Jamie—"

She stood up straight and planted her feet. "I'm just like you!" she cried at him. "What if I'm gay?"

"Lesbian?" He came close to her and stood facing her, very serious. "Homosexual? Any particular reason you should be?"

"*You* are!"

"I wear a size thirteen shoe too. That doesn't mean you have to. Are you having sexual feelings about girls? About Kate, maybe?"

"No! That's disgusting!" Then Jamie realized what she had said. Was it disgusting that Bridge loved David? She felt herself flush deep red. But Bridge was laughing and hugging her.

"You're fine," he said, kissing the side of her head. "I give you a one-in-ten chance, same as anybody else. Do you like boys?"

"Not really." Jamie blushed harder.

"Are they disgusting too?"

"Kind of." Though there was this one boy in art class that Jamie looked at a lot.

"Good attitude. Keep it a few more years. Sis, you never cease to amaze me."

"Why?"

But he just grinned and hugged her again, then let her go. "C'mon. You can help me."

"Huh?"

"Just c'mon, before everybody gets up." He was prowling so early for a purpose, then? Evidently. He strode to the little white toolshed at the bottom of Shirley's yard—a former outhouse, actually—unlatched the door and reached in for—a shovel?

"Oh, no. Did a turtle die?" Jamie hoped not. It was too soon for another funeral.

"No!" Bridge gave her a startled glance. "No, nothing died." He hesitated, then his voice grew soft. "Something's alive."

"Huh?"

Bridger propped the shovel against the shed as if he needed both hands to show her something. But then he grew very still, just standing there, looking back at her. Almost shy. Almost afraid.

"Bridge?"

The way he stood with his hands not quite touching, his mouth not quite speaking—it was as if he were holding his breath. Or praying.

Slowly he reached into his jacket pockets. He extended his hands toward her. Half a dozen brown, inert objects lay in his palms.

"Flower bulbs?"

In a low voice he said, "Resurrection lily bulbs."

Jamie gawked at him.

"You thought it was just Ma's name? So did I, up till a few weeks back." Bridger handed the bulbs to Jamie and picked up his shovel again, turning toward it, Jamie sensed, mostly for an excuse to turn his face away. "David showed me in a catalog. It's a real flower, called the resurrection lily. It comes up in the springtime, this big cluster of bright green leaves. But then they die, the whole thing dies, there's nothing there—until August, when all of a sudden a stalk shoots up." Bridge pivoted and faced her. "Then it flowers. A big, dusky-pink lily flower."

Jamie looked down at the drab, onionlike objects in her hands.

"So, anyway," Bridge said very softly, "of course I had to get some, and Shirley said I could plant them here. I've been trying to settle on a spot. Can't seem to make up my mind."

Jamie knew why. He really, really wanted them to grow. They had to go in just the right place.

"How about outside the fence?" Jamie suggested. "Away from the trees? They'll get sun and rain, and the turtles won't dig them up or eat them."

Bridger stood a moment as if listening to the air, then nodded and gave her a glance that said thanks. "See, I knew I needed you. I'm a city boy. I don't think of these things."

Once they selected a place, it didn't take Bridger long to dig up a short trench, laying the sod to one side, loosening the dirt underneath. Jamie sat and watched, not talking, letting Bridger alone. The earth looked rich and loamy—good garden dirt. Once Bridger was satisfied with his flower bed, he laid the shovel aside and knelt down on the ground. "Want to stick some in?"

He tried to sound very casual, but Jamie knew he was not casual about this at all.

She started at one end of the trench with three bulbs, and Bridge started at the other end with his three, and they met in the middle, neither of them saying a word. They covered the bulbs, patted down the loose dirt and replaced the grass sod on top, then just sat there like a pair of kids making mud pies.

Jamie knew why her brother had bought the bulbs, why he was planting them here. "So you think Mamaw can do that?" she teased gently. "Flower late? Come to life again when it looks like she's finished?"

"I hope so." But he did not look up, and she realized with a jolt that he was crying.

"Sorry," she whispered.

"You didn't do anything." He wiped his face with his sleeve, then looked at her, getting his smile back. "I'm fine. Never mind me. Stupid flower names. I'm just glad she didn't name you Daisy, and me Bud or something."

He made Jamie laugh out loud, and he laughed with her. How could he do that, laugh when he had just been crying?

He laughed, and lay back in the grass. The world smelled good, like rich dirt. A turtle, Burp, supervising the activity from the other side of the fence, peered at Bridger then swung its head to eye Jamie. Bridge eyed her too, smiling his warm, slow smile.

"Don't ever quit, Sis," he said.

"Huh?"

"Ever since the first day I met you, you've been looking for Jamie Bridger. Did you find her yet?"

Jamie momentarily choked on the joke of everything, then grinned.

"Well, did you?" Bridge insisted.

"No." Then Jamie thought of all that had happened. "Well, yes. Kind of. Some days." She thought of all the things she still wanted to do and know and find out. "Not yet. I'm getting there."

"Keep getting there," Bridge said.

"Till I'm a hundred, you mean?" A breeze blew like the earth breathing. In a minute Shirley would come out and bang on her kettle, and the turtles would do their slow, slow dance. Bridge lay mellow in the grass, Mamaw would rise up and paint flowers, and Jamie wanted to keep it all forever in her sketchbook. She smiled, because for that moment she knew who she was—kind of. Maybe she would be a world-class artist, maybe not. But when she was a hundred and fourteen years old, she wanted to be heading down the road in a white Ferrari, still young, still going somewhere, looking for Jamie Bridger.

[Fic]
Spr   Springer, Nancy.
        Looking for Jamie
        Bridger

DATE DUE

[Fic]
Spr   Springer, Nancy.
        Looking for Jamie
        Bridger

DATE	ISSUED TO
JAN 8 '97	Nicole 5
JAN 29 '97	Kari Oneto 8
SEP 7 '98	melissa wright 8
	kavleigh Loth 4